THE LITTLE CHRISTMAS WAIF

Victorian Romance

FAYE GODWIN

PERSONAL WORD FROM THE AUTHOR

DEAREST READERS,

I'm so delighted that you have chosen one of my books to read. I am proud to be a part of the team of writers at Tica House Publishing. Our goal is to inspire, entertain, and give you many hours of reading pleasure. Your kind words and loving readership are deeply appreciated.

I would like to personally invite you to sign up for updates and to become part of our **Exclusive Reader Club**—it's completely Free to Join! I'd love to welcome you!

Much love,

Faye Godwin

CLICK HERE to Join our Reader's Club and to Receive Tica House Updates!

https://victorian.subscribemenow.com/

CONTENTS

PART I

CHAPTER 1

VICKEY COOPER HAD OFTEN HEARD the rich folk who came to stay at her mistress' manor house talking about the "Christmas Spirit." They used words like *jolly*, and *festive*, and talked about how everything was *magical*.

Even though it was two weeks before Christmas right now, that magic felt a very long way away. Kneeling by the kitchen grate, Vickey blinked back tears as she polished away, her fingers numb with cold and exhaustion. Her knees ached on the cold stone floor, and there was a draft blowing in under the back door that whistled around her threadbare uniform.

She was eleven hours into a fourteen-hour day, and tiredness was making her hands tremble. Gritting her teeth against the cold that turned them numb, she felt a shiver run through her as she worked at the grate, trying to bring it to some kind of a shine. It made no sense to her that her mistress, rich dowager Miss Watson, had decreed that every single grate in the entire house needed to be polished by Christmas. It wasn't as if any of the rich guests she entertained – ladies in fine silk and men in neatly cut suits – would ever dream of setting foot in this kitchen or any other. She wondered if any of them even knew what a raw potato looked like.

But Vickey knew, and there was a mound of potatoes waiting for her by the kitchen sink that would have to be peeled and chopped in the next hour for Miss Watson's dinner. It would be a miserable task in the biting cold of the kitchen. Even though she could finally light a fire in this hearth when the polishing was all done, it would take ages to warm the enormous room. She had to hold back tears. There wasn't even a chance of taking some rest on Christmas Day itself – Miss Watson would have a lavish party, and it would be the busiest day of Vickey's whole year.

In fact, Vickey was quite ready to make up her mind that Christmas was the worst time of year when a little giggle danced through the air like sunlight on rippling water. She couldn't help smiling as she sat back on her heels for a minute, looking over her shoulder at the blanket she'd spread out in the corner.

"Now what are you up to, Cara?" she asked softly.

The child on the blanket looked up, striking Vickey as she always did with her nearly angelic beauty. Shining locks of russet-brown hair poured over her shoulders, their grubbiness unable to hide their bounce and radiance. Freckles were scattered like fairy dust over her pert little nose, which turned up at the end as delicately as a flower petal, and she had tremendous dark eyes so large and so limpid that they put Vickey in mind of some deep well of fresh, cool water.

"What are you giggling about, my little hummingbird?" Vickey asked.

Cara beamed at her, her plump cheeks rising adorably against her eyes, chubby with toddlerhood despite the fact that her arms and legs were stick-thin for want of good food. "You so pwetty, Mama," she said, the fat syllables sliding off her clumsy baby tongue.

"Pretty?" Vickey let out a short laugh. She knew she had Cara's dark eyes, but as she glanced at her reflection in the glass of the silverware cabinet to her left, they looked like hollow pits in her pinched and pale face. "Mama doesn't feel very pretty right now."

"You pwetty," Cara repeated. She stumbled on uncoordinated legs to the edge of the blanket, then hesitating, plopped down again. It was the housekeeper's rule more than Vickey's: if Cara was outside of the tiny room she shared with her mother, she had to stay on her blanket. Vickey didn't mind. The very fact that she got away with having Cara there at all continually surprised her. Most days, she still feared she would be dismissed. And where else would she be allowed to have her daughter with her?

"I hungry," Cara added.

The ray of sunshine in Vickey's heart was blotted out instantly. Cara was always hungry.

"Oh, baby," said Vickey, putting down her rag. She went over to the blanket and scooped the little girl into her arms, cuddling her close against her cheek. Cara's body was unwashed, but when Vickey pressed her face into the soft little neck, she still had a sweetly baby smell.

Cara giggled. "You tickle," she said.

"I do, do I? Well, I wasn't even trying," said Vickey, her voice rising in playfulness despite herself. She switched her grip on Cara so that she could tickle her right under the armpits. "*Now* I'm tickling."

Cara was squealing in glee. "Mama! Stop!" she gasped breathlessly, tears of mirth running down her rosy cheeks.

Laughing, Vickey set her down, but it was a mistake. Cara was overexcited. Bouncing around Vickey's feet, she held up her small hands, her eyes dancing. "Catch me, Mama," she cried. "Catch me."

"Cara, no!" Vickey gasped.

She saw the disaster coming before it happened, but there was no way for her to stop it. As Cara ran across the floor, her bare feet slapping on the stone, the door to the scullery swung open and a scullery-maid stepped through it. A huge tray in her arms was stacked high with china so delicate that Vickey could nearly see through it, edged in gold, painted in meticulous navy patterns.

"Cara!" Vickey was shouting.

Still running, her brown hair streaming down her back, Cara looked around. Her laughing eyes were fixed on Vickey and not on the heavily-laden maid in front of her. The maid let out a gasp, stepping back, and the stack of dishes teetered horribly on the tray. Vickey lunged to grab her child, but it was already too late. Just as she thought the maid might save it yet, Cara ran headlong into the girl's legs.

The maid gasped, stumbled, juggled the tray frantically, and somehow managed to keep her grip on it – but a delicate little soup bowl toppled from the top of the tray. With her arms around Cara, Vickey could do nothing but watch as it plummeted to the ground and shattered into a million tiny, expensive shards that spread out over the stone floor like broken ice.

The sound of it shook her whole world. She stared at the scullery-maid, wide-eyed, and the girl's eyes were filled with fear.

"*WHAT* is going on down there?"

The roar came from just upstairs – the housekeeper's domain. Cara had gone very quiet in Vickey's arms; Vickey cringed alongside the other maid as the heavy sound of wooden clogs on the stairs echoed like the approach of an enemy legion.

Mrs. Mackerel, the housekeeper, swept into the kitchen with the ferocity of a battleship, her cardigan billowing like a great mainsail. Her bright red nose glowed between the twin circles of her spectacles, which made her grey eyes seem colder and harder than ever. When they rested on the shattered bowl that lay on the floor, they narrowed dangerously, flashing like metal.

"What is this?" she hissed. "A broken dish, two weeks before Christmas?" She rounded on the scullery-maid. "That dish is worth more than a year's wage for you, Polly."

"S-s-sorry, Mrs. Mackerel," Polly squeaked.

Cara gave a little whimper. Vickey backed away, clutching her.

"Still, I have no doubt that this particular disaster wasn't your fault, for once." With frightening suddenness, Mrs. Mackerel spun around, facing Vickey. She extended a long, trembling finger to point at the child in Vickey's arms. "YOU."

Vickey clutched Cara instinctively. "Ma'am..." she began.

"Save your babbling, you foolish wench," Mrs. Mackerel all but bellowed. "You've been nothing but trouble ever since you came here, running around with that dreadful young cab driver, and look where it's gotten you." She gestured at Cara.

"I don't see why Miss Watson turns a blind eye to that child, but I'm telling you, Vickey, she knows about every single one of the costly little incidents that brat has caused."

"She's j-just a little child," Vickey whispered, cuddling Cara, whose shoulders were beginning to shake with silent sobs. "She doesn't know any better."

"That's exactly why she doesn't belong in this kitchen," hissed Mrs. Mackerel. "I suggest you get rid of her – or teach her some manners, before I do." She clenched a fist under Vickey's nose. "It's only two weeks to Christmas. You can't afford to have any distractions."

The woman stomped out of the kitchen, and the scullery-maid gave Vickey a wide-eyed look before hurrying out of the room. Vickey allowed herself to collapse to the floor beside the shattered remnants of that stupid china bowl. Cara cuddled into her lap, crying outright now in fear, her small hands clutching Vickey's dress. Burying her face in the little girl's hair, Vickey sobbed with her.

Christmas really was the most miserable time of the year.

CHAPTER 2

EDNA HALL TOOK a sip from her wine glass that lasted perhaps a little too long. She lowered it slowly, noting the judgment in her sister's eyes as she sat in the comfortable leather armchair by the hearth. The firelight danced on Giselle's half-moon glasses, but she had them balanced on the end of her long nose, making it easy to peer at Edna over the top of them.

Edna tried to look casual as she lowered her wine glass to the little table by her chaise-lounge, carefully arranging her hands on top of her skirt, feeling the hardness of the hoop just beneath the flowing silk. "Thank you very much, Gizzy," she said. "That was a most excellent luncheon."

"You know I don't like to be called that," Giselle snapped.

"Oh, but you're my sister," said Edna. "I can give you a little pet name, surely? I've been calling you that since we were children."

"We're not children anymore." Giselle tipped up her nose.

Edna decided to let it go. She leaned back in the chair, careful to avoid allowing her corset to pinch her, and gazed into the fireplace. It danced and flickered, casting a golden light on the wreath over the mantelpiece, which was punctuated by holly and mistletoe.

"Thank you for inviting me," said Edna, and her gratitude was genuine despite Giselle's sourness. "My house always feels cold and empty to me, but with Glen away on business for the next two days, well, it's just unbearable." She passed a thin hand over her face. "I don't know how you stand to live alone."

"I don't live alone and neither do you," said Giselle. "We both have armies of servants."

"Oh, Gizzy, but you know what I mean," cried Edna.

"I don't think I do," said Giselle. "I'm always glad of my own company." She shot Edna a pointed look. "I'm grateful Papa left everything to me when he died so that I wouldn't have to marry some rich businessman like you did."

"Giselle," countered Edna. "I love Glen. He's a good, kind man."

"You love his money, too," said Giselle tightly. "So did Mama – that was why she encouraged you to marry him."

Edna sighed. "Much good it did her," she said quietly. "At least she died without knowing that she'll never have any grandchildren."

Giselle gave Edna a look that told her to be quiet, but Edna couldn't help it. Her anguish spilled out of her the way it always did, bitter on her tongue. "Oh, I don't know what I'm going to do, Giselle. I *have* to have a child – I simply must. But Glen and I have been married for seven years and still I have nothing to show for it. I just want to hear a little child's laughter in that big old house. I want to be a mother so badly it... it consumes me."

"So you've said at every dinner party and every family gathering since you were married," said Giselle dryly.

Edna felt tears filling her eyes. She let them spill over despite the expensive powder on her cheeks. "But you don't understand, Gizzy, what a dreadful thing it is to be a barren woman. I'm so ashamed I can barely show my face in public, and every time I hear a baby crying, I feel I will go mad unless I have that sweet little thing in my arms. Oh, oh, oh, I don't think I can survive another childless Christmas."

"How I wish you wouldn't carry on so, Edna," said Giselle impatiently. She lifted her wine glass. "Have another sip to settle your nerves."

Edna was shakily raising her own glass to her lips when the sound of small feet came pounding up the hallway. She froze, her eyes wide, hardly believing her ears. A little girl's laughter rang like sleigh bells along with the pattering feet, and she blinked, wondering if she was hallucinating. A child? In Giselle's house? She lowered the glass slowly. Was she having a vision?

The next moment, a little girl rushed into the room, and Edna realized that it *was* a vision – a vision of an angel, or at least, the most beautiful cherub that Edna could ever have imagined. Despite the grey rags that draped off the child's thin shoulders, she was the loveliest little thing that Edna had ever seen. Her hair wrapped around her like a cloak, looking chocolate brown at first glance, but where the firelight glanced off it, threads of scarlet shimmered in it like bronze. Her eyes were enormous and dark and limpid, and they widened as she gazed up at Edna and Giselle, skidding to a halt with her grubby toes in the thick carpet.

"Oh," exclaimed Edna.

"Ugh," groaned Giselle. "This little thing again." She made a shooing motion with a hand that flashed with jewellery. "Go away."

The child was frozen to the spot. She gazed up at them, her full pink lower lip quivering.

"No, stop!" cried Edna. "Don't chase her away. Oh, she's the loveliest little thing. Who is she, Giselle?"

"A mistake," snapped Giselle. "The result of a wayward kitchen maid who doesn't have any idea of morals. I should have gotten rid of the little brat long ago, but truth be told, I forgot all about her until the last few weeks. She's started to make a dreadful nuisance of herself." She got up from her chair, her chins wobbling. "I'm going to have that maid's head for this."

"Don't frighten the child," said Edna. "She's so beautiful." She held out a hand to the little girl. "Hello, darling."

The little one dragged her eyes away from Giselle, turning them to Edna, whose heart turned over immediately. She could feel herself melting on the inside as the child's features relaxed into a breath-taking smile. "Hello," she said, her piping little voice musical to Edna's ears.

"Leave the child be, Edna," snapped Giselle. "I'm sure she has lice."

Running feet sounded in the hallway again, but this time, they had the heaviness of an adult. Edna looked up from the little girl just as a thin young woman – hardly more than a girl herself – appeared in the doorway. She stopped short when she saw Edna and Giselle, and her pinched face drained of what little colour it had had in the first place. She was a skeletal creature, draped with an ugly uniform too big for her.

"You!" Giselle thundered, rounding on the young woman. "What do you think you're doing, letting your offspring roam around my beautiful house like this? You've been nothing but trouble ever since you first came here. Why, you've destroyed more things in my house than you've ever even cleaned, you worthless little hussy."

The girl's eyes were locked on the child. "I'm s-sorry, Miss Watson," she whispered.

"I'm sure you are – and you will be even more so when I've halved your wages again," Giselle spat venomously. "I should turn you out onto the streets, you and this result of your wantonness. How dare you allow this child to have the run of my house?"

"I'm so sorry, Miss Watson," the girl whimpered. "I only took my eyes off her for a minute. I'll just take her and – and go." She reached for the child's hand.

Giselle hesitated, and Edna saw something cold and calculating in her sister's eyes. As the girl gripped her child's hand, Giselle spoke. "No. I don't think so," she said.

The girl looked up, her eyes frightened. "Excuse me, ma'am?"

"You're clearly incapable of disciplining your own child," said Giselle coldly. "I think it's time she learned a lesson from me." She put her hands on her hips. "Sit her down in that corner over there – and she must sit there quietly until your return at the end of your shift. If not, she will be punished."

The girl's eyes were sparkling with tears now. She looked at Giselle, then back at the little child, who was gazing up at her without comprehension. Edna knew that any form of defiance would result in the young woman's immediate dismissal.

So did the young woman. She ducked her head. "Yes, Miss Watson," she whispered. "Cara, darling – come here." She led her over to the corner Giselle had indicated. "You're going to sit down here for a minute for me, darling. Just play quietly – and don't move, all right?"

Cara seemed completely unfazed, smiling up at her mother. "Yes, Mama," she lisped, sitting down contentedly.

"Now go," barked Giselle. "And don't come back until I give you leave."

"Yes, ma'am." Head low, shoulders shaking, the young woman fled the room, leaving the toddler alone in the corner.

Giselle let out a gusty sigh. Without a glance at Cara, she threw herself back down on her armchair and took a sip of her wine. Edna's eyes were on the little girl, who was sitting contentedly on the floor, playing with the hem of her threadbare dress. She was so pretty... Edna couldn't forget the sound of her laugh.

"Do you want her?"

Edna startled, looking up at Giselle, who was studying her in her usual sharp way.

"Excuse me?" Edna said.

"The child," said Giselle impatiently. "Do you want the child?"

"What do you mean?" said Edna.

"Are you stupid as well as barren, sister?" Giselle demanded. "You want a child. Well, I don't know anything about children, but that one seems fairly healthy and normal enough. Why don't you take her?"

"Take her?" Edna echoed. "I couldn't do that." But even as she said it, she knew that she could. Oh, she not only could, she desperately longed to sweep that little girl into her arms and cuddle her and carry her all the way back to her house. She'd give her everything, she'd give *anything* to have that angelic child.

"Why not?" said Giselle shortly. "The mother needn't know what happened. The child's just in my way, and I'd prefer that to dismissing the mother who's a good worker."

"I... I don't know." Edna let out a long sigh, thinking about the way that the young woman had looked at that little girl. She'd looked at the child like she was her whole world. The way that Edna would have looked at a child if she'd been able to bear one in her womb, to bring it forth into the world, to nourish it from her own body, to hold it in her arms and see herself in its eyes...

"What would Glen say, though?" Edna said, dragging her eyes away.

Giselle waved a dismissive hand. "You'd just have to get around Glen," she said. "He knows you want a child. Tell him that you got her from the workhouse as a Christmas surprise. No one will ever know about this – we'll just have to hold our family gatherings at your house for a while, until the child grows too big to be recognized."

Edna bit her lip. "I still… I'm not sure."

"Is it the girl you're worried about?" Giselle snorted. "Oh, Edna, don't let her bother you. She brought the poor thing into the world without having any way to provide for it. This little child has no future at all – I'd be surprised if she even survived to adulthood with that kitchen maid raising her. I can't possibly keep the maid on with the child, and if she's dismissed, she'll never find work again. They'd both starve on the streets."

"Maybe… Well, yes… In truth, it would be doing them both a kindness," said Edna slowly. She reached a hand toward the girl, then brought it back to her chest, clutching it in a fist against her heart. She imagined all the things she'd do for that little girl if she brought her home. Oh, she'd give her all the toys she could ever dream of, and a wonderful warm nursery with a great window and books with pretty pictures in them and a soothing painting on the wall. She'd nurture the child, and read to her at night, and appoint a governess who would dress her in fine clothes and teach her how to enunciate each syllable and host a dinner party. She'd watch her grow into a gloriously beautiful young woman. She'd plan her wedding. She'd bounce her grandchildren on her knee…

"Oh... oh," Edna breathed, clutching her fist more tightly to her chest, feeling that she had to hold herself together or the expanding force of her longing would blow her into fragments. "Oh, Giselle, do you think I could?"

"I think you *should*," said Giselle shortly. "It'd solve a lot of problems for me − assuming you want her. She's got lice, I'm sure of it, and she hardly looks like she's been washed in all her life. Why, she can hardly speak, and she's more than two or three years old."

"Oh, that's not true, is it, honey?" Giving in to the thickening tide of her love and yearning, Edna crossed the floor and knelt down by the little girl. "Hello," she said. "You can talk, can't you?"

"Yes, I can," said Cara brightly.

"Your name is Cara, isn't it?" said Edna.

"Yes," said the child. "Who you?"

Edna held out her arms. Without a moment's hesitation, Cara scrambled into them, giggling as she pressed her hands into the softness of Edna's silk skirt. "Soft. Shiny," she gasped, enraptured.

"Don't you worry, pretty Cara," Edna whispered. Her mind was racing with justifications, but her heart was already made up as she wrapped her arms around the child, around *her* child. "I'm going to take very good care of you."

CHAPTER 3

Vᴵᴄᴋᴇʏ ᴛɪᴘᴛᴏᴇᴅ ᴅᴏᴡɴ ᴛʜᴇ ʟᴏɴɢ, dark passage, horribly aware of every squeaking floorboard and every tap of her feet. She held her breath, desperate not to make a sound. The murmur of voices was coming from the dining room; slow voices, the voices of people who had eaten their fill and were relaxing in front of a fireplace now.

Vickey couldn't remember a time in her life when she'd ever eaten her fill. And right now, her veins throbbed with anxiety and tension. It had been hours since she'd left little Cara sitting on the floor of the parlour with Miss Watson and that other woman, and even as she'd walked away, she'd had a terrible feeling in her heart. Miss Watson, she knew to be cruel; and that other woman... She'd had more softness to her than Miss Watson, but it was the wrong sort of softness. It felt loose and unbalanced.

Like she couldn't be trusted.

That had been just after lunchtime. Now, dinner had been enjoyed and Miss Watson's guests were settling down to conversation around the fireplace, and still Vickey hadn't heard a peep from Cara. Something was off. She could feel it. Something wasn't right.

Vickey knew she'd be dismissed for roaming around these upper rooms for no good reason, but that was nothing compared to losing her little girl, her sunshine... her hummingbird. Cara had earned the nickname because she was forever warbling away, humming a little tune, singing, chattering to herself. It sounded as cheerful as the hum of a tiny, bright bird fluttering from one flower to the next.

Vickey buried her face in her hands. She couldn't be without Cara.

The creak of a door to her left made her jump, cowering back under an oil painting of some royal relative of the Watson family. The dining room door swung open, and Miss Watson strode out in all her finery, yards of shining silk and finest lace wrapped lavishly around her figure. She hesitated, her eyes resting on Vickey for a moment. They were as cold as ever, and they made Vickey tremble to her very soul.

She expected Miss Watson to scream at her and chase her off. Instead, the woman slowly closed the door behind her, then folded her arms—rings and bracelets sparkled as she moved.

"I suppose you're looking for that brat of yours," Miss Watson said.

Vickey summoned her courage. She barely had the strength to even look Miss Watson in the eyes, but for Cara, she'd do anything. "Please, ma'am," she said, trembling. "If you'd tell me where she is, I'll fetch her right away, and you'll never have to see her again. She'll never break anything again either."

"Oh, I have no doubt of that," said Miss Watson icily.

Her tone of voice made Vickey's blood freeze. "Where... where is she?" she whispered.

"I don't know," said Miss Watson.

Vickey swallowed hard. "W-what do you mean?"

"I mean exactly as I say, and I say exactly what I mean," snapped Miss Watson. "I don't know where the child's gone. One minute, Edna and I were talking, and the next, she'd run off. She just disappeared." She shrugged. "I doubt you'll ever find her."

Vickey stared into Miss Watson's eyes, horror filling her veins with something that felt like frozen treacle. The woman had to be lying. She *had* to be. But what would she have done with Cara? Where would a little girl like that go?

"Cara wouldn't run away," Vickey managed. "She wouldn't..."

Miss Watson's hand flashed out, rings sparkling, more suddenly than Vickey was ready for. It rang across her cheekbone with blinding impact, a bejewelled ring crunching into her skin. Vickey staggered back against the wall, letting out a gasp of horror as she clapped one hand to her bleeding face.

"Are you accusing me of being a liar?" Miss Watson hissed.

Vickey's skull pounded. "N-no, ma'am," she stammered.

"Good answer." Miss Watson lowered her hand. "Now be off with you and get out of my sight. Be grateful you have a place to lay your head – and that this won't be a Christmas on the streets for you."

Stunned, Vickey stumbled off, feeling the warm blood coursing down her cheek. Her heart boiled with fear and hatred.

Where was she? Where was her little girl?

CARA HAD NEVER BEEN on such a grand adventure in her life. The lady with the lovely soft dress – she'd heard grumpy old Miss Watson calling her Edna – had hair that was even softer than her dress. It was in wonderful curls, and while Edna had been talking with Miss Watson, she'd let Cara sit on her beautiful dress and play with those glorious curls all she liked.

She was twisting the long strands of honey-golden hair around her fingers when Edna's arms wrapped around her. Cara liked hugs, but she was a little surprised when Edna stood up, lifting Cara into her arms. It was a bit uncomfortable; she would have preferred to sit on Edna's hip, like she always did with Mama. She squirmed, trying to get into the right position, but Edna clutched her very tightly. Almost as tightly as Mama had done yesterday when Polly had dropped the dish.

"Don't be afraid, my little darling," Edna said. "We're going to go for a lovely ride."

"A wide?" said Cara, forgetting her discomfort as she gazed up into the pretty lady's face. It looked like she had gotten some flour on her cheeks; she must have been crying, because her tears had washed some of it away.

"Yes, darling," said Edna. "A ride in a carriage."

"What's a... a ca... a cawwiage?" Cara managed.

"Oh, it's a beautiful thing. It's so comfortable to sit in, and it goes wonderfully fast. Let me show you," said Edna.

Cara was excited to see the carriage. "Can Mama come too?" she asked.

Edna's grip tightened on her, and something in her face changed. "No," she said, in the firm voice that Mama used when she really wanted Cara to be quiet. "She can't."

Cara knew better than to argue with that voice. "We go see?" she said, hoping to make pretty Edna smile again.

"Yes." Edna's face lit up. "Let's go and see the carriage, my little love."

Cara had never seen the front of the house before, and she stared around in awe as Edna carried her – sideways in her arms, like a baby – through the tall hallways and down winged staircases that led to marble floors that shimmered like the fresh snow that lay thickly on the streets outside. She gasped in delight, gazing up at a wonderful, glittering thing that hung high above them.

"Is that Heaven?" she asked.

"Oh, darling." Edna laughed. "You say such silly things. That's just the chandelier."

Cara didn't know what the word meant, but it sounded so pretty. Maybe it was a step to Heaven, or something they could climb on that would take them there. Would the *carriage* be as pretty as that?

When they stepped out of the front door, Cara gave a little gasp of cold. The wind was frigid, hurling snowflakes against her that pelted on her skin. She threw her arms around Edna's neck, cuddling close to her warmth. Edna let out a soft sound – something that seemed half sob, half sigh, the way Mama did when Cara snuggled her. It sounded so sad, but Mama always said that it was a happy sound.

"Don't worry, sweet, sweet little girl," Edna murmured. "The carriage is nice and warm."

Lifting her face from Edna's chest, Cara looked up and gasped in delight. The carriage was beautiful. She'd seen things like it before, speeding up and down the street when Mama took her out for a walk or to visit Granny, and she'd seen people getting in and out of them. Mama had never told her its name, but she'd always wanted to take a ride in one. Two splendid horses – dapple grey, with great yellow plumes that waved in the breeze were harnessed to it.

"Oh," cried Cara. "Go fast."

Edna laughed. "We can go as fast as you like for that beautiful smile of yours, darling."

There was a man standing beside the carriage, wearing a pretty red-and-blue suit just like the broken toy soldier that Mama had found on the street for her, and he pulled the door open to reveal a warm interior all red and pretty. Edna stepped inside with Cara in her arms, then set her down against the opposite window. It was wonderfully warm, and the cloth was so soft that Cara had to press both hands into it for a moment, enjoying it.

The door slammed shut, and Edna put an arm around Cara's shoulders. "Do you like it?" she asked.

"Yes," said Cara.

Edna laughed. "Home, Patrick," she called.

The coachman made a clicking sound with his tongue, and suddenly the carriage was moving. It made a happy, rattling sound as it moved, and the horses' hooves rapped out a cheerful tune on the road. Cara giggled with glee, looking out of the window, and gasped in delight when she saw how quickly the houses and streets were flying past. This was a hundred times faster than walking. Why had Mama never taken her on a carriage ride before?

"I like it. I like it." Cara giggled, clapping her hands.

"That's wonderful," beamed Edna.

Cara gazed up at her, cuddling close to the pretty lady in her soft, soft dress. "You nice," she whispered.

Edna looked away, the way Mama did when Cara said something wrong. She was very quiet for a moment. "I don't know about that," she whispered.

Cara wasn't sure what that meant, but she did know that the carriage ride was plenty of fun. She pressed her hands against the window, watching the snowbound world glide by. Everything was covered in brightness: candles shone golden in the windows, holly wreaths decorated every door and window, and even the smiles of the people passing by seemed to be all gleaming and gorgeous.

"Why everything so pwetty today?" she asked.

"Oh, because it's nearly Christmas, honey," said Edna.

Cara gazed up at her. "What's Chwistmas?"

Edna leaned over, kissing her cheek quickly. "Goodness, have you forgotten? Or have you never known? Well, no matter. You'll soon find out – and you'll learn it's the very best time of year," she said.

The carriage was coming to a halt, and when the toy-soldier-man opened the door, Edna held out her arms to Cara. "Shall we go and see my house," she said.

"Your house?" Cara felt a bolt of worry. She drew back. "But I want to go home."

"This is your home now, darling," said Edna.

"No," said Cara. "My home's with Mama."

Edna's eyes flashed suddenly, the way Mrs. Mackerel's did when she was angry. "Not anymore, Cara," she said sharply. "I don't want to hear you talking about your mother again."

"But I want Mama." Cara's heart was hammering. "I want my mama."

"I'm your mama now," snapped Edna. She grabbed Cara's arms. "Do you hear me? I'm your mama."

"No!" Cara shrieked, yanking her hands away. "Want MAMA."

But Edna was too strong for her. Already she was dragging her out of the carriage and into her arms, marching up to the gaping doors of a huge, dark house, much bigger than Miss Watson's. "You can scream all you want, Cara, especially with Glen being away," she said firmly. "You're mine now."

"MAMA!" Cara screamed, her voice echoing in the great hallway. "MAMAAA!"

CHAPTER 4

HUDDLED in the corner of the marketplace, Vickey watched morosely as shopkeepers began to move around, adjusting the Christmas decorations in their windows. There were hand-written signs in almost every window announcing special prices or discounts due to the season; holly wreaths hung on every door, and candles burned in all the windows. A few of them were humming Christmas carols. It all made Vickey want to scream.

She'd never liked Christmas, but she'd never imagined that this one would turn out as appalling as it had.

It had been nearly a week since Cara, the light of Vickey's life, had so mysteriously disappeared. Despite the fact that she knew losing her job would mean homelessness in the dead of winter, Vickey had thrown herself into making every effort to find her child. Miraculously, so far, she hadn't been tossed onto the street.

She'd spoken to everyone she knew, suspicious of that soft-eyed woman. She just knew that she must have had something to do with Cara's disappearance, but no one seemed willing to help her. No one wanted to tell her who the woman even was – which made tracking her down all but impossible.

Vickey took a deep breath, clutching her courage with both hands, as she gazed across the marketplace to the tall figure standing in the far corner. Growing up on the streets had seldom given her good experiences with the police, but the bobby standing on the corner now was her only hope of finding Cara. Stately in his long coat, the polished emblems flashing on his hat in the meagre morning light, he was the picture of strong authority.

Authority had never treated Vickey well, but now, she didn't have a choice. She'd do whatever it took to get Cara back.

Summoning her courage, Vickey set off across the market-place, her hands buried deep in the pockets of the threadbare uniform that was the only dress she owned. The bobby was ignoring her completely, his eyes trained on a pair of urchins creeping around the front of the bakery, and she had to clear her throat twice to get his attention.

He turned around, a pair of bright blue eyes over a sandy moustache surveying the bruises on her face. "Sorry," he said, turning away. "I'm too busy for your domestic dust-ups."

"It's… it's not that, sir," Vickey stammered out, trembling with fear and the cold. "I need help."

"So do we all," said the policeman. "Go away."

"Please, sir." Vickey swallowed hard. "My little girl's gone missing. I think she's been taken."

The man turned, raising an eyebrow. "Taken, you say?"

"Yes, sir, yes she has," said Vickey, "and I think I saw the woman who did it. She was a guest of my mistress, and she was looking at my little girl in such a way that – well, it frightened me, sir."

The policeman raised both eyebrows. "What does your husband say about it?" he asked.

There it was. The thing that had made her an object of hatred and vitriol since little Cara was born. Tears filled her eyes as she backed away. "I don't have a husband, sir," she whispered.

The policeman snorted, turning back to his observation of the street urchins. "Then you brought this on yourself, wench," he said. "I'm not going to solve your problems for you. Why, if we had to run after every illegitimate child that disappeared from a drunken mother's arms, we'd have no time for murderers or thieves."

"Sir, please…" Vickey began.

The policeman turned, raising his truncheon in a way that left no question about his intent with it. "I told you to go away," he snapped. "I won't ask again."

Blinded by tears, Vickey turned and ran, sobbing hopelessly. Did no one care that her beloved Cara, her precious Cara, her heart and soul, had gone missing? Did no one care about catching that soft-eyed woman who'd been so frightening?

Vickey had hardly slept for the last week, spending every hour she could away from work as she combed through the neighbouring gardens and knocked on the servant's entrances of every house on their street, asking if anyone had seen a beautiful child with red-brunette hair and dark, sweet eyes. No one wanted to help her; those who tried hadn't seen anything. For everyone else in Miss Watson's household, life seemed to be going on as normal. As if the very heart of Vickey's world hadn't been brutally ripped out of it.

The manor house was just a block away. Wiping her eyes on her apron, Vickey tried to calm herself, knowing that she had to put a brave face on it to keep her job. Working at the manor house was her best way of finding the woman – maybe she'd come to visit Miss Watson again.

But as she turned the corner and walked up the narrow path through the servant's door, Vickey's heart plummeted into her shoes. Mrs. Mackerel was standing at the doorway as if waiting for her, her powerful arms folded in triumph, chin jutting out like a bowsprit.

"There you are," she said, her voice dripping with savage glee. "I'm surprised you decided to come back at all."

"I'm sorry, Mrs. Mackerel," Vickey began. "I was just..."

Mrs. Mackerel stepped back, reaching behind the door. A moment later, a bag sailed through the air, scattering things everywhere: a handful of the coins Vickey had saved, a pocket Bible, Cara's spare dress. They splattered on the snow, and Vickey stared at them, then back at Mrs. Mackerel.

"I can't tell you how much pleasure it gives me to say this," said Mrs. Mackerel. "Go. Get out of here. Never come back to this house again."

Vickey stared at the objects again, uncomprehending. "W-what?"

"You're dismissed," said Mrs. Mackerel. "Goodbye."

She stepped back inside and slammed the door, leaving Vickey alone in the cold garden to scrabble for her few belongings in the snow as tears coursed down her cheeks.

She was utterly and completely alone.

CHAPTER 5

A THIN, wailing cry tore through the house just as Edna raised the first spoonful of soup to her mouth. Freezing in place, Edna closed her eyes, willing the cry to be nothing but her own imagination. She'd heard it so often over the past week, maybe she was beginning to imagine it…

No. Glen was also putting down his spoon now, and the cry came again, ringing through the dining room from upstairs.

"Edna." Glen looked over at her, his eyes a mixture of confusion and anger. "What on earth is the matter with that child? Surely it's not normal that she should be crying all day and night like this."

Edna looked into Glen's gentle grey-blue eyes, shining under his mop of sand-colored hair. Even though her late mother had chosen Glen for her more than Edna had chosen him for herself, she'd still never regretted marrying this strangely tender man, successful though he was. It hurt her deeply to lie to him, but she knew that if he knew the truth about Cara... It didn't bear thinking about.

"I told you, darling, she's been through so much," said Edna. "Her mother dying in the workhouse must have been terrible for the poor little soul. I just had to have her. We can't let the poor thing suffer so."

Glen's eyes softened, and he passed a hand over his face. "I know, my love," he said with a sigh. "I just can't stand the sound of her crying all the time. You'd better go to her, considering we still haven't found a nanny and probably won't until after New Year's Day."

Edna nodded, slinking away from the supper table even though guilt was burning through her belly. It felt like a living thing that was sinking its jaws into her, eating away at one piece of her after the other. Why was she so afraid of telling Glen the truth? Because she knew he'd be angry with her.

Worse still, she knew he'd tell her what she'd really known all along: that she'd done something horribly, horribly wrong to take little Cara away from her real mother.

She let out a sigh, mounting the steps up to the nursery they'd rushed to put together for their new family member. Her heart felt so filled with regret that she could hardly breathe past the swollen, aching weight of it.

CARA HAD WOKEN up all alone in the strange, big room, almost as big as the kitchen back at home. Edna kept telling her that this was her room now, but she didn't want it. She didn't want a room so big that it felt like there might be anything lurking in one of the many dark shadows, or even in the terrifying wardrobe. It towered in one corner, covered in carvings that may have been meant to be flowers or leaves, but by the slant of streetlight that came in through the great window, they looked like angry faces or reaching hands that might grab her from her bed at any moment.

The bed was soft, but softness wasn't what Cara was looking for. She wanted warmth; she wanted the smooth presence of Mama, to hear the thump-thump of her mother's heart each time she wrapped her arms as far around Mama's body as they would go and pressed her ear close to her body.

There was no one in this bed with Cara. It was nearly as big as their entire room had been, and she felt lost in it, like she might sink down into its softness and simply disappear forever. The only reason she ever fell asleep in it was because sometimes she cried so much that her eyes ached and could no longer stay open.

Now, she was awake, and the room was huge and empty and so, so dark. The only light she could see – except for the cold streetlight in the window – was a crack of gold around the great door. She scrambled out of bed, her heart racing, feeling those eyes in the wardrobe glaring at her. She could almost hear the skittering of little clawed feet on the floor, chasing after her, coming to get her.

"Mama!" Cara was terrified, and she missed her mother so much that her bones ached. She ran to the door, but she couldn't manage the knob. "MAMA!" she screamed, sobs ripping through her little body. A cascade of tears began to pour down her cheeks; she could feel the blood rushing in her ears. "MAMA. MAMA. HELP ME! HELP ME!"

Her hands pounded on the door, fingernails scraping on the wood, but she couldn't reach the knob, and she knew that the shadows were coming for her...

Suddenly, the door burst open. Cara fell headlong on her face, her hands smacking down on soft carpet. Warmth and light spilled around her, and for a heart-stopping instant, she thought that it had happened at last. That Mama had come for her at last... But when Cara sat up, lifting her face to the light, the face that glared down to her had none of Mama's pinched prettiness. Instead it was soft and white and rounded and framed by honey-gold curls.

"E-Edna?" Cara stammered. She sat up, still sobbing. "Where's Mama?"

"Oh, Cara, how many times must I tell you this?" Lately, Edna's voice was sounding like this more and more often: short and snappish, nothing like the soothing tones she'd used the day that she and Cara had met. "I'm your mama now. I don't want you to call me Edna. It's rude – I'm your mama."

"You not," Cara cried. "Mama is Vickey."

Edna's face twisted in a way that made her look ugly. "Well, she's not here, and you'll never see her again," she snapped. "You're my child now, and you'll call me Mama or else."

Cara was so confused. Why didn't Mama come to get her? Why had she let Edna take her away? And how could Edna want to be called Mama? There was only one mama. You couldn't have two mamas. Could you? Cara didn't know; all she really knew was that she wanted her mother's arms. The thought made her cry all the louder, and suddenly, Edna's hand closed on her upper arm like a claw.

"Stop that!" she barked, shaking her. "Stop that this instant."

Cara had never been shaken before. She didn't like it; it hurt her arm and made her teeth rattle. Turning instantly silent, she stared at Edna, frightened.

"There." Edna's hand relaxed a little on Cara's arm, and there was something softer in her eyes, like she felt a little bit sorry. "You can't keep on crying like this, Cara. You're upsetting the whole household. We've given you a lovely room and clothes and toys." Edna touched one of the two thick braids that now held Cara's hair, each ending in a silky curl. "That's no way to treat us, is it? You shouldn't just yell and scream at us like this."

"Mama," Cara whispered. "I want Mama."

"*I'm* your mama," snapped Edna. "And if I hear you ask for that woman one more time, I'll shake you until your teeth rattle."

Cara didn't want to be shaken again, but she didn't want to call Edna by the wrong name, either. There'd only ever be one Mama. Afraid of being shaken, she just nodded her head.

"That's a good girl," said Edna. "Now let's get you back to bed."

Cara submitted to having her hand taken and followed Edna back into the big room. And she wondered why Edna would take her away from Mama only to be so cross and mean to her all the time.

CHAPTER 6

"Here, Patrick," said Glen. "You can pull up the horses right over here."

Glen's coachman was a tall, grizzled old man who'd been serving his family since Glen could remember, and he was a quiet type, never questioning. But as he looked up at the staid pillars of the workhouse at the end of the street, doubt crossed his face. "The workhouse, sir?" he asked.

"Yes. I won't be long," said Glen.

Patrick's flicker of interest seemed to have faded. He reined in the horses in silence, and the footman hurried to open the door.

As Glen stepped out of the carriage, a swirl of snowflakes played around his ankles, sending cold fingers poking up the legs of his tailored trousers. Buttoning his coat, Glen suppressed a shiver, and not because of the cold. He'd grown Papa's business so much that he'd elevated his family's status from respectably middle-class to decidedly upper-crust, and he'd never been this close to a workhouse before. Why would he? This place was for poor people.

He could nearly taste the desperation that hung in the air around it. It made him tremble a little for some reason. The rest of town, on this bright Christmas Eve, was all alight with decorations and well wishes and music; but this place seemed untouched by any kind of Christmas spirit. It seemed untouched by any spirit at all; the very air that hung around it seemed cold, and damp, and broken, and heartless.

Maybe this wasn't such a good idea. Glen hesitated, staring up at the imposing facade, listening to the hubbub of voices from within. He'd been so desperate when he'd left the house a few minutes ago. That child, Cara, was sobbing hopelessly in the nursery; Edna was doing the same, her head buried in her hands as she flung herself across her bed. It was gut-wrenching for him to watch, and not only because his wife's sorrow was breaking his heart. She was a silly thing at times, but he loved her, and he hated seeing her like this. But he also felt terrible for that poor little girl.

Glen bit his lip. No. He had to do this. Edna wanted a child – *needed* a child, in a deeply primeval way that he couldn't hope to understand, but having Cara was doing no good at all. His wife needed a happy, playful child. An older one, he'd decided, and a boy, too. They were more adaptable than little girls, he hoped. Maybe she'd forget about Cara and let her come back to the workhouse again if he brought her a child that would love her. It'd even be better for Cara, he was sure; nothing could be worse for that poor child than crying constantly the way she was doing right now.

Squaring his shoulders, Glen walked up to the great doors, noting that there was no sign of any Christmas decorations on them. A porter – a ragged-looking creature in a dirty uniform – watched him with little interest. "You lost, guv'nor?" he said.

Glen kept his distance from the grubby little man. "No, my good man, I'm quite sure of where I am," he said primly. "I would like to speak to the matron."

The porter raised an eyebrow. "It's Christmas Eve," he pointed out.

Glen sighed. He may never have spoken to a workhouse porter before, but he knew this drill. Reaching into his coat, he pulled out a silver shilling and held it out. "I would like to speak to the matron," he repeated, a little more firmly.

The porter's eyes widened. He reached for the coin, and Glen closed his hand. "The matron," he said.

The porter gave him a vengeful look, but nonetheless turned around and slouched off into the workhouse. Glen blew on his hands, feeling the cold despite his gloves. Christmas Eve was beautiful, he thought, looking down the long street as snowflakes came tumbling down, sparkling in the streetlight. Still, he wouldn't want to be one of the unhappy souls that spent it on the street – or in this great grey ice-box of a building, for that matter.

At least one child would be able to come home to a warm house and all the love that Edna could give him.

The door swung open again, and a powerfully-built woman with a hooked nose and crooked fingers stepped out, her starched collar nipping at her wrinkled neck. "What do you want?" she said sharply, her colourless eyes raking him without respect.

"Ah, madam." Glen nodded to her. "I would like to adopt a little boy."

"On Christmas Eve? Go away." The matron turned.

"I can make it worth your while," said Glen hastily.

She looked over at him, her eyes calculating. "A boy?" she said. "What for? Chimney sweeping? Factory work?"

Glen felt his stomach clench at the thought of the many children who were traded like cattle, put to work in trades too rough and dangerous for grown men. "No," he said, allowing his disapproval to leak into his tone. "To raise as our own child." He smiled. "Just the same as the little girl that my wife came for, a few weeks ago."

"Your wife?" said the matron, without much interest. "Who's that?"

"Edna Hall," said Glen. "Didn't you recognize the carriage?"

"Can't say I did," said the matron off-handedly, gazing beyond him to the carriage.

What does that mean? Glen wondered. Edna must have gotten Cara at this workhouse. The only reason why he and Edna even knew where this workhouse was, was because they passed by it on occasion on the way to the milliner's that Edna favoured. Where else would she have gotten the child?

The matron was eyeing him suspiciously. "Look, mister," she said, "I'm more interested in my Christmas feast than in you, so gentleman or not, you can wait a few days and adopt a child when the workhouse is less short-staffed."

"I'm afraid this can't wait." Glen placed a hand in his pocket and shook it so that the matron could hear the promising jingle of coins. "I need that child right away, as a Christmas surprise for my wife. A little boy – not too small, but young enough to settle into a new home." He hesitated. "And not one that has a habit of crying too much. I want this to be easy on my wife."

The sound of the coins had reduced the angry-eyed matron instantly into the model of subservience. With a simpering smile, she nodded, almost curtsying. "Well, my dear sir, I believe I have just the child for you," she said. "He's a hard worker, very well-behaved, and only five years old. Both parents died in an accident – there won't be any relatives bothering you about him."

"That sounds perfect," said Glen. He took out a fistful of coins. "Bring him right away."

As the matron hurried off, he could only hope that he was doing the right thing. He couldn't let the weeping Cara ruin Christmas for Edna.

EDNA WAS SILENTLY grateful that Cara had chosen this day to be quieter than usual. She knelt down, checking the buttons on the little girl's thick fur coat, and sighed as she looked into those deep, wide eyes. She was still such a beautiful child, so enchanting. Edna wished with all of her heart that Cara could be the little girl she'd always dreamed of.

But she wasn't. It had been two weeks to the day since she'd brought Cara home, and all the child had done was cry and cry, beg for her mother, and cry some more. She was even thinner now than she had been when Edna had fetched her from Giselle's house; the little cheeks were pinched and pale, and her eyes looked bigger than ever in her shrunken face.

"Oh, Cara," Edna murmured. "I wish you'd just be a good girl."

Cara studied her with those giant eyes, saying nothing. Edna sighed, pulling a knitted hat down over the child's ears. She hated to send her back into the ragged life she'd had before, but at least she could make sure Cara would be warm for a winter or two before she outgrew the fine clothes that Glen had bought for her. It was better than making Glen suffer through a Christmas Eve filled with her crying.

"All right, darling," said Edna, relenting. "You know what to tell everyone, don't you?"

Cara stared at her. Edna prayed that the girl was understanding. "You tell them that I found you wandering on the street," she said, "and that I dressed you warmly and brought you straight back home. Don't tell anyone you stayed in my house, all right? Not a soul. It'll be our secret."

"Our secret," Cara repeated tonelessly.

"Come on, now." Edna wrapped her fingers around Cara's limp little hand. "Let's get out."

The footman pulled the door open, and Edna helped Cara down, setting her feet gently on the pavement in front of the house. She was watching Cara's face as the little girl laid her eyes on the manor house that had been her home for so long, and she saw how her dark eyes suddenly lit up, the colour returning to her pinched cheeks.

"Mama!" Cara cried, yanking her small hand free of Edna's.

"Cara!" Edna called. But the little girl was deaf to the world. She took off, her little legs flying under her fine new clothes, disappearing around the back of the house toward the servants' entrance, and Edna's shoulders slumped. It was just as she'd expected. Despite the love and adoration she'd lavished on that little girl, none of it had mattered. Cara just couldn't understand that Edna had been trying to do her a favour.

A burst of bitterness shot through her heart. "Well, then, do as you please," she muttered angrily to herself. "Go back to your sad little life and your bleak future. I would have given you the world on a silver platter if only you'd loved me."

Sighing, Edna turned away and stamped up to the main doors. The footmen opened them graciously; they all knew her well. Even though she knew it was appalling manners, she found her own way up the staircase and right to the door of Giselle's study.

She rapped on it twice.

"Go away," called Giselle. "I'm reading."

"It's me," said Edna. "Your sister."

There was silence from the study, and Edna pushed the door open. It was a cosy, velvety, cluttered room, the walls adorned with expensive art, a fire crackling busily in the massive hearth; Giselle was at the centre of it behind her desk, reading from a huge gold-leaf tome. It was scandalous that a woman should be in a study such as this one – their father's old study – but Giselle had long since stopped caring about scandal.

She glared at Edna over her glasses. "I should have you know, I'm having a party tomorrow," she said. "I need my rest."

"I wouldn't be here at all if it wasn't for your lack of good judgment," snapped Edna.

Giselle waved a careless hand. "What do you want?"

Edna folded her arms. "That child – Cara. She's... not settling into our household."

"I could have told you that much," said Giselle, turning back to her book. "You should have just been content with your lot, the way I am."

Edna gritted her teeth, chafed, as always, by her sister's manner. "Well, I'm not," she said, "and that's why I've brought her back."

It was the first time in her life that she'd spoken so boldly, and it was worth it to see the shock on Giselle's face as she looked up, the colour draining from her cheeks. "You've done *what?*" she cried.

"I've brought her back," said Edna. "Don't worry – I've told her to tell everyone that I found her on the street. No one will know what happened. She'll be back with her mother by now – she took off toward the servants' entrance – and we can forget about this whole dreadful affair."

Giselle glared at Edna for a long, cool minute. Then, with studied calm, she took off her glasses and laid them aside.

Edna felt judged. "It's for the best," she said. "Cara did nothing but cry all the time. She'll be happier now."

"Oh, so you're doing this for the child's sake?" said Giselle, picking up her book again. "I'll have to disappoint you, in that case."

"What do you mean?" said Edna.

"Her mother is gone."

"Gone?" Edna laid a hand on her chest, a horrible suspicion filling her mind. Had the grief of losing Cara killed that poor young girl?

"Dismissed," said Giselle. "She was most insufferable. Searching everywhere for that child. I couldn't stand the sight of her anymore."

Edna's heart hammered. Cara's mother was gone, and she was wandering around the servant's quarters all alone. She spun around and rushed out of the hallway, leaving her pompous sister to her reading and her judgment.

CHAPTER 7

EVERYTHING WAS SO GLORIOUSLY familiar as Cara ran into the massive kitchen. Its great flagstones, its wonderful warm fire, the cheerfully bright surface of the stove, the strings of onions hanging from the ceiling – it was home. It was her home, and it was where Mama lived.

Cara's heart was hammering with excitement. She couldn't wait to see Mama, to look into her lovely dark eyes again, and feel herself being caught up in those gentle arms and held close against her mother's soft chest. She'd tangle her fingers in the greasy strands of Mama's hair even though they weren't soft and bouncy like Edna's. She'd hear Mama's voice, saying things she understood, things that understood her. And everything would be all right again. The world would be back to the way it was supposed to be again.

"Mama!" Cara cried, skidding to a halt in the kitchen. Which way would she go first? The scullery, or the sleeping quarters? "Mama," she called again, then ran through the narrow door and into the thin hallway between their rudimentary rooms. She knew the way by heart, choosing the fourth door on the left without having to count them, rushing toward it. Mama would be on the bed, wrapped in a blanket, and she'd sweep Cara into her arms and they'd fall asleep cuddling close...

Cara thumped the door open with both hands and stood in a perfectly empty room.

The bed was still there, but the blanket was gone. The little cracked vase that Mama had kept on the windowsill, always with a little flower or just a sprig of something green in it, was nowhere to be found. The box that contained their clothes was empty.

And there was absolutely no sign of Mama.

Cara was aware that her heart was hammering deafeningly in her ears. "M-Mama?" she whispered, hearing the hope in her own voice, but she knew that something was wrong. Something was very, very wrong.

Mama had left without her. Maybe she thought that Cara didn't love her anymore. Maybe she was angry, and she'd gone away. In that cold and bleak moment, Cara knew that she would never see her mother again.

Her legs felt like water. They folded under her, and she covered her face with her hands, sobbing with all of her heart. Mama didn't love her anymore. No one did.

There were footsteps in the hallway, light and swift. Cara raised her face, feeling her heart thump. She knew those footsteps, and they didn't belong to the woman she'd known as her mother, but she knew them, nonetheless. And perhaps there was still a place for her to find love in this icy world.

The footsteps hesitated outside the door. "Cara?" the voice called.

Cara ran out of the little room, and Edna was waiting there with her shiny dress and her wonderful soft curls, looking too bright and brilliant to be in this spartan place. Her eyes were wide and frightened, until they rested on Cara and filled with relief.

"Oh, darling," Edna sighed. "There you are."

Cara ran to her, holding out her arms. She saw surprise in Edna's eyes, felt her hands trembling when they closed around Cara's chest and swept her up. Edna held her tightly, and Cara buried her face in those lovely soft curls, inexpressibly glad to feel an embrace – any embrace.

"Oh, darling, I was so frightened," she breathed.

Cara heard the fervency in her voice and felt the warmth in the way she was being held, and she felt her whole heart reach out toward this woman, knowing she was the only warm place left in Cara's entire world.

She wrapped her arms tightly around Edna's neck. "Mama," she whispered.

Edna sighed, pulling back to look into Cara's eyes. "What did you say?"

Cara rested a hand on Edna's cheek. It was inexpressibly soft, and she smelled wonderfully like flowers.

"Mama," she repeated, looking into Edna's eyes.

They filled immediately with tears. Edna pulled her close, pressing her lips to Cara's cheek.

"That's right, little one," she whispered. "Mama. I'm your mama now."

For the first time, Cara had no choice but to believe her.

❧

CARA FELT EXHAUSTED. She leaned her head on her new mama's shoulder as she mounted the steps to the house – to what was now Cara's only home.

Mama laid a hand on Cara's hair. "Wake up, darling," she said. "You don't want to sleep through your first real Christmas Eve, do you?"

Cara lifted her head groggily. She'd heard her previous mother talking about Christmas before, but it always sounded horrible and busy, like it was far too much work. "Too tired for Chwistmas," she murmured.

"Don't be silly, love," said Mama. "There's going to be delicious food, and beautiful presents – and just *look* at what the servants have done in the hall."

Mama sounded excited, so Cara lifted her head to stare, and her heart flipped over. She'd seen a Christmas tree before, of course, in shop windows, but those had been nothing compared to this magnificent thing that towered over a whole corner of the hall. It sparkled with beautiful, shiny baubles; a glittering golden angel adorned the very top, and the rest of it was wrapped in something that shone like moonlight and adorned in brightly colored red-and-white things that looked like shepherd's crooks.

"Pwetty," Cara gasped.

Mama carried her over to it. "And tasty, too." she said, taking down one of the canes. "Taste this."

Cara was a little surprised, but she happily thrust the end of the ornament into her mouth. It was wonderfully sweet, melting on her tongue. "Candy," she gasped, delighted.

"Yes, candy." Mama kissed her cheek. "And that's not even the best thing about Christmas."

"Edna?" Glen, Mama's husband, called from the front door. "I'm home – and I have a surprise for you."

Mama set Cara down at the feet of the Christmas tree, spinning around as her eyes lit up. "Oh, darling, you won't believe what happened today," she sang out.

Glen put his head around the doorway. He was grinning, his gentle green eyes sparkling. He'd never said much to Cara, but she'd always liked him; he seemed kind enough even though he never knew what to do with her. "And I can't wait to hear all about it, love," he said, "but first I want to show you what I've gotten you for Christmas. I think it's the best gift you've ever had."

Mama giggled like a scullery-maid, clasping her hands in front of her. "What is it?"

Glen stepped aside. "Come inside, Levi," he said.

A little boy walked through the doors and into the beautifully decorated hall, and he looked instantly like he belonged there. Dressed in a little tweed coat and polished little shoes, he was a few years older than Cara, with walnut-brown hair combed carefully to one side with a perfect parting down the middle. Yet, when he took a step forward, she saw his eyes flash around the room like he was hiding his fear. He seemed uncomfortable in his shoes – perhaps, like her, he wasn't quite used to them yet.

Mama stared from the boy to Glen. "What's this?" she gasped.

"A child for you," said Glen, "from the workhouse." He bit his lip, half nervous. "He's a sweet boy, so quiet, and I thought…" His eyes darted to Cara, and he stopped. "His name is Levi," he said at last.

"Oh." Mama had both hands clapped over her mouth. "Oh… Levi. What a beautiful name. And what a beautiful child." All at once, she rushed across the polished floor and swept Levi up into her arms; he pressed his hands against her shoulders to stop himself from falling face-first into her chest. When she kissed his cheek, though, he quietly submitted, even though his eyes were wary. "Oh, Levi, you're so lovely," she said. "I'm going to be your mama, and you're going to be my boy. My beautiful, beautiful, perfect little boy."

She glanced back at Cara with a wide smile. "Come meet your brother," she urged.

Cara felt sick. She didn't have a brother. She wasn't sure anymore whether she even had a mama. Not a real one. She shook her head, digging her feet into the carpet. Edna's expression hardened. "Come meet your brother," she said again, impatience in her tone.

"I want my mama," Cara said, her stomach twisting with a terrible feeling of dread and loss.

Edna stiffened. She glared at Cara. "Too good to be true," she muttered. Then she sniffed loudly and turned back to Levi.

"Mama," Levi uttered, and Edna clasped her hands together in glee.

There was little that Cara could do other than stand by the Christmas tree and watch. Yet there was a part of her that knew she was losing her mother for the second time in a single day.

❧

CHRISTMAS EVE WASN'T AS miserable and horrible as Cara had expected it to be, but it did go on for a very long time. There were a lot of good things to eat, and even more new toys (Cara hadn't even known that there were this many toys in the entire world), and everyone was singing and happy, but it was very late by the time Cara was finally led back to the giant nursery.

It was different, too. Someone had brought a small cot into it and pushed it up against the window; when Cara headed for the bed where she'd always slept, Mama stopped her.

"No, Cara," she said. "That's Levi's bed now."

So it was that when the clock struck midnight on Cara's third Christmas, she was lying wide awake in the unfamiliar cot, staring up at the ceiling and trying very hard not to be afraid. She'd learned now that her old mama didn't want her anymore; she'd been so glad that her new mama had been here for her. But everything was different now that Levi was here.

He'd been very quiet at the table, eating carefully with his knife and fork, saying "please" and "thank you" all the time, and never asking for a second helping. Now and then he'd glanced over at Cara, but she tried her best not to look at him. Instead she looked at Mama, and almost all night, Mama looked adoringly at Levi.

It was as if Cara didn't really exist.

She rolled onto her side, staring at the great four-poster bed that she'd never wanted, and at the little lump that was Levi's body under the soft sheets. She could just make out the shadow of his hair lying on the pillow; he had his back to her, and she watched him breathe, and wondered what it meant. She didn't like sleeping all alone in that big, scary bed, but she didn't know what it meant that her new Mama had moved her to this cot.

Did it mean that Mama didn't love her anymore, either?

She felt a hot tear run down her cheek. Confusion twisted through her. Downstairs, she could still hear the adults talking; it sounded like someone was singing a Christmas song. Those songs were all about joy and jolliness. Cara wondered if the people who made up those songs had ever had a Christmas like this one, so lonely, so confusing, and so frightening.

A quiet little sob escaped her, and there was a rustle from the four-poster bed. Startled, Cara froze, pulling her sheets up to her nose. Levi had turned over, and in the twilit room, he was watching her. She could just make out the flash of the whites of his eyes.

"Are you crying?" he said.

Cara pulled her covers over her head. "No," she lied.

She heard the rustle of his blankets being pushed back, the quiet pad of his feet on the floor. A small hand tugged at her covers. "Why are you crying?" he asked.

Cara lowered the covers a little, so that she could just see over them. Now that Levi was close to her, he smelled of soap, and for the first time she saw the colour of his eyes even in the semi-darkness. They were a deep, dark brown, soft and limpid as the eyes of Glen's pointers, and there was something warm and honest and friendly about them that made Cara want to trust him.

She sat up. "I'm afwaid," she said.

"Why?" asked Levi.

"My old mama didn't want me anymore," said Cara. "Now I don't know if Mama want me." She felt the tears welling up again.

"Perhaps it doesn't matter who wants you, or doesn't," said Levi. "Look around. It's warm here and safe, and there's lots of food." He held out a little hand to her. "It's better than a workhouse, anyway."

Cara took his hand in her own chubby, sweaty fingers, and felt a little better. "I don't wanna be alone," she whispered.

"You don't got to be alone," said Levi, his gentle eyes shining. "I'm here with you now."

PART II

CHAPTER 8

Five Years Later

Levi's eyes shone under his knitted hat, his gloved hand held aloft, a round snowball glimmering between his fingers. Cara giggled as she peered at him from behind the trunk of one of the towering pine trees that surrounded the great lawn in front of the Hall house. His eyes were darting this way and that as he searched for her, but what he didn't know was that she'd laid a false trail across the lawn, then doubled back by swinging from one low branch to the next, barely touching the ground.

She stifled another giggle as Levi followed her footprints, passing right by her, his snowball still poised to throw. When he was a few paces away, Cara struck.

"HA!" she cried, a yelp of triumph, and leaped out from behind the trunk. Levi turned around just as Cara launched the snowball in her own hand. It sailed through the winter air, glittering, and hit him full on the forehead. Snow scattered everywhere, and Levi gave a laughing yelp of surprise and annoyance.

"You sneaky little thing," he cried, wiping snow from his eyes. "I'm coming to get you."

Cara gave a happy shriek as Levi rushed at her and ran away, her shoes crunching on the snow, her too-short dress flickering around her ankles. The cool wind kissed her cheeks, Levi's laughter was flying beside her, and at times like these she could forget the great gulf that had been ripped between them. She could forget how Mama took care of him but not her. She could forget how he stayed in the main part of the house and she stayed in the kitchen quarters.

"Got you," cried Levi, his voice rising with triumph, a split second before his snowball hit her in the back of the head. Shattering harmlessly against her hat, it was still enough to tip her just slightly off balance. Cara's feet skidded on the snow. The next thing she knew, she was face-down in snow, spitting it out as she sat up. She wasn't sure if she was gasping for breath or just breathless with laughter.

"Oh dear!" Levi's warm hand closed over her arm. "Are you all right?"

Cara let him help her to her feet, grasping his arm for support. "Yes, yes," she panted. "I'm fine. The snow was soft."

"You were going pretty fast," Levi laughed. He dusted the snow from the front of her dress. "I didn't think I was actually going to hit you."

Cara giggled. "Your aim's pretty good, but I think mine is better."

"Oh, you do, do you?" Levi said, straightening out her hat. When the light was crisp like this, and he was happy, his eyes shimmered a rich, warm hazel. "I suppose we'll have to have a rematch and find out."

Cara grinned. "I like that idea."

"Levi!"

Both children flinched as if feeling the lash of a whip across their shoulders. Cara ducked her head, knowing immediately she was in trouble, and Levi took a step back from her. Peering from underneath her lowered eyelids, Cara saw Mama standing on the front steps of the mansion. The passing years had changed her; she was paler these days, and her rich golden locks were now streaked with silver. If Cara thought hard, she could remember playing with those pretty locks, running her fingers through their silken strands. That must have been a long time ago. She couldn't imagine Mama lifting her up onto her hip now.

"Yes, Mother?" Levi called dutifully, folding his hands behind his back.

"Come inside," Mama ordered. "Cara, what are you doing on the lawn? Get back to the kitchen at once."

"Yes, Mama," Cara called.

She watched Mama's mouth twist bitterly, the way it always did when Cara called her that. Why? She remembered, vaguely, that there was a time before Mama and the Halls' house. She'd called someone else by that name then, but she knew that this new Mama – Edna – had insisted that she was now Cara's mother. So why did it annoy her so much to be called Mama?

"I'd better go," said Levi. He touched Cara's shoulder briefly with a snow-dusted mitten. "I'm sorry."

"See you later," said Cara hopefully.

Levi grimaced. "If I can get away."

He scampered off toward the house, and Cara wrapped her coat more tightly around her shoulders before trudging off across the lawn to the thin path that led to the servants' entrance. She was never allowed to use the great double doors at the front of the house anymore.

When she pushed open the narrow servant's entrance and walked into the kitchen, the glorious smells of Betty's cooking surrounded her, making her feel warmed up from the inside.

The kitchen was enormous; the hearth alone was big enough for Cara to stand up in, which she knew because it was often her job to polish the grate. It crackled merrily now, and the stove on the other side of the kitchen was hard at work, with savoury-smelling pots bubbling on its cast-iron surface.

Betty was at the long table, chopping carrots with brisk, expert movements. Her expression was as sour as ever when she saw Cara walk in; her pursed lips made her look like she was permanently sucking on something, and judging by the frown that perpetually wrinkled her brow, it was something bitter. Yet when her pale blue eyes rested on Cara, there was kindness in them.

"Where have you been, child?" she demanded. "You'll catch your death out there."

"I was playing with Levi," said Cara. She went over to the table and grabbed the bowl of carrot peels to tip them into the compost bin. "We were having a snowball fight."

"Snowball fight, eh?" Betty grunted. "That's a boys' game."

"Levi says most of his friends have gone off on holiday to the seaside," said Cara. "He doesn't have a brother, so he has to play boy games with me."

"Right well he does, poor mite," said Betty. "Stuck-up old Mrs. Hall hardly gives him a moment to himself." She hurled the chopped carrots into a pot of boiling water with unnecessary violence. "Bring me seven potatoes, there's a good girl."

Cara fetched them from the bag in the pantry, carrying them close to her chest before she laid them on the chopping board. "What are you making for supper?" she asked.

"Roast fowl and vegetables for the mistress' family," said Betty. "We're just having yesterday's soup tonight, I'm afraid. I'm busy boiling fat for suet – there's no time to make a proper supper for the servants."

Cara sighed, sinking down on the little mat in the corner by the stove where she spent her nights. She tucked her thin blanket around her legs and looked up at Betty. "I used to eat with Mama and Glen and Levi," she said.

Betty gave her a sharp look. "That was a long time ago, girl," she said. "I'm surprised you even remember. Why, apart from that first Christmas that you came to this house, I've been feedin' you every Christmas since."

"I know it was a long time ago," said Cara meekly, folding her hands in her lap. "I just remember it, that's all. Mama gave me a dolly." She looked up at Betty. "Why did they make me come to sleep down here in the kitchen?"

Betty shifted uncomfortably, although her eyes were on the potatoes she was peeling. "Well, child, I suppose Levi got too big to be sharin' his room with a little girl," she said. "He needed the nursery to himself."

"But there are so many other rooms in the house," said Cara. "I could have stayed in one of them." She looked away. "I don't think Mama wants me anymore."

Betty sighed, setting down the potato, and leaned her hands on the table. Looking over at Cara, her tone was sharp, yet sad.

"Well, you're right in that," she said. "She made that much clear when she ordered you to sleep down here in the kitchen. But there's no need to cry over spilled milk. You have somewhere warm to sleep and food to eat, so keep your chin up, that's what I always say. And besides, you have old Betty, don't you?"

Cara got up from her mat and hurried across the floor to fling her arms around Betty's waist, hugging her closely.

"I know I have you, Betty," she whispered. "And I love you very much."

"Oh, do get out of the way, you silly little thing," grumbled Betty. But Cara felt a gentle arm encircle her for a brief moment.

CHAPTER 9

IT WAS the next morning before Cara could see Levi again. Even though his governess had gone on holiday, and Levi didn't have to spend hours studying every day like he used to, Mama still seemed determined to keep him busy. When Cara was out in the vegetable garden pulling up frozen carrots or taking out the rubbish, she saw him going down the great stairs, all dressed up in his finest and his hair combed neatly to one side, heading for the waiting carriage. He told Cara that he despised the dinner parties and dances that Mama dragged him off to, but according to Levi, he had no choice but to go.

It was a lovely day and Betty was up to her elbows in plum pudding; she'd chased Cara out of the kitchen, telling her to play outside by the stables and get out from under her feet. Cara was more than happy to oblige. The sunshine was sparkling brilliantly on the shimmering snow that covered the cobbled stable yard; the horses were all peering over their half doors, blinking as snowflakes settled on their long eyelashes. They all wore canvas rugs, and Cara thought it must be inexpressibly warm in their deeply-bedded stalls. She was afraid of their great iron-rimmed feet, though, so she stayed in the yard, avoiding the stable lads as they shovelled out the snow.

The horses had been picking at their hay racks, and the wind had caught a few bits of hay and blown them across the yard. Cara gathered them up strand for strand, then wandered from one loose box to the other, offering each horse a strand of hay – except for Glen's big black stallion, which tended to bite.

"No," she told the stallion, who kicked at the door of its stall. "You can't have any. You're horrible."

"Oh, he's not horrible," said a welcome voice from within one of the stalls. "He's just spoiled, that's all."

"Levi," cried Cara, hurrying over to the stall at the far end of the block. Levi's perky-eared Welsh pony whinnied when he saw her, and a moment later, Levi's face joined the pony's over the half door. He was grinning, his hair mussed, his fine suit flecked with horsehair.

"Hello." he said. "I was just about to come looking for you in the kitchen, but I know Betty can be quite frightening in plum pudding season."

"She made me come and play outside," said Cara. "I thought Mama had taken you somewhere for breakfast."

"Yes, to frumpy old Aunt Giselle's house." Levi pulled a face. "She's so dreadful, I don't know why Mama ever sees her. Still, she's agreed to come to our Christmas dinner, unfortunately."

Cara sighed, leaning her elbows on the stall door as she fed the bits of hay to Levi's pony. "I wish I could come to Christmas dinner," she said quietly. "I don't remember much about Christmas dinner, but I watch through the window sometimes, and everyone seems so happy. The hall looks beautiful, and there are crackers on the table, and everyone seems to get presents."

"It must be really hard to see all that delicious food being cooked, and then never get a chance to eat any of it," said Levi.

"I've never even tasted standing beef rib, even though I know how to help make it," said Cara. "I... I wish I could come to Christmas dinner."

Levi put a hand over hers where it rested on the stall door. "Maybe you will."

"What do you mean?" said Cara. "Mama doesn't even let me sleep upstairs anymore. She'd never let me come to Christmas dinner."

"Ah, but you see, you're forgetting that it's *Christmas* dinner." Levi grinned. "And Christmas is a very special time of the year."

Cara stepped back, folding her arms. "No, it isn't," she said. "Not when you have to work four times as hard in the kitchen, and when it's terribly cold every single night, and when you don't get any feasts or presents or cards or any of those nice things. Why, we don't even have a Christmas tree. Betty says it would only get in the way."

"That's all true," said Levi, "but what's also true is that Christmas is a time of miracles."

Cara felt her eyes widening. "Miracles?"

"Yes," said Levi. His eyes were shining with excitement. "Wonderful, wonderful things can happen at Christmastime, Cara. We've been hearing all about it at church and in school, and Mama keeps telling us about it. See, things can happen at Christmas that don't happen at any other time of the year. Impossible things." His grin split his face. "*Wonderful* things."

"Like... like Mama taking notice of me again?" said Cara. She felt her heart turn a magnificent little cartwheel of hope.

"Exactly like that," said Levi.

Cara swallowed hard, trying to choke back the trembling feeling of joy in her gut. "So perhaps Mama will call for me this Christmas," she said. "And I could sit next to you at the feast. And maybe I'd even get a present. And come to sleep upstairs again. And learn to read and write like you."

"Oh, if I could have any miracle this Christmas, I'd hope it'd be that one," said Levi, with a long sigh. "We'd be able to play together all day long, and do our lessons together, and then I'd have someone to talk to when Mama drags me off on one of her visits."

"I'd like that," said Cara. "I'd... I'd *love* that."

She'd more than love that, she thought, as Levi bounded out of the stall and suggested a game of hide-and-seek in the loft. She'd change her mind about Christmas forever, if only this one could be beautiful.

CARA BIT her tongue absently as she leaned over the huge, steaming pot. Betty had poured off the boiling water, but it was still very hot as she reached in with a ladle and scooped out a few of the rich, dark chestnuts within. She tipped them into a bowl and grasped one between her thumb and forefinger. Heat seared her fingertips, and she yelped, dropping it again.

"Give them a little time to cool, you silly girl," said Betty, who was sweating at the kitchen table, wrestling with an enormous turkey as she worked lard over its slippery skin. "You'll burn your fingers clean off like that. Chop the salt pork while you're waiting."

Sucking her burned fingers, Cara turned away from the pot and went to fetch the kitchen knife and the salt pork can. She was just emerging from the pantry when there was a clattering of feet outside, and Levi burst into the kitchen, his cheeks rosy red, hair mussed by the thin wind that blew outside. His dark hair was dusted with snowflakes, which melted as Cara watched, like morning stars fading on a brown sky.

"Levi!" she cried, delighted to see him.

"Levi?" said Betsy, staring at him with hands covered in lard. "What are you doing here? Your mother will have my hide if she sees you in here, that she will."

"Oh, don't worry about Mother, dear Betty," said Levi. "She's twittering up and down the house about the decorations and other such silly things. I could hardly stand it anymore. Christmas dinner will only be this evening." He grinned. "I'd much rather help you all down here."

"Help?" Betty grunted. "I've never seen a man who was any *help* in the kitchen."

"Oh, don't chase him off, Betty, please," Cara begged. "Let him stay. He'll be good. I like having him here." *Besides*, she thought, *maybe if Mama calls for him, she'll remember me. And then I'll sit next to Levi at the table and taste a bit of turkey for the first time in my life.*

"All right," grumbled Betty. "Sit yourself down on the stool by the fire, young master, and see to it that you don't get in my way."

"Yes, ma'am," said Levi playfully, planting himself down on the stool.

Cara started chopping the salt pork, carefully avoiding her fingers. It was a good thing that Levi had come down to the kitchen. That meant that Mama hadn't called him up to get ready for dinner yet – which meant that there was still time for her to suddenly remember that she had a daughter, and to call Cara.

"I can't wait for the feast," she told Levi, setting the chopped salt pork aside to be made into stuffing later. Testing a chestnut, she found that it was cool enough to touch, and started rubbing it between her fingers; the boiled skin fell away easily, and she tossed the nut into a bowl. "I've never had turkey before. Or chestnuts. Or plum pudding."

"Plum pudding isn't nice, but I love turkey," said Levi.

Betty looked up sharply from the turkey. "What makes you think you're going to taste it now, Cara?" she demanded.

Cara felt abruptly shy. Lowering her eyes, she focused on the chestnuts, getting every bit of skin off them. "Oh... well... nothing," she murmured.

"I know something's been on at you the past few days, Cara," said Betty. "You're like a rich child on Christmas Eve – a child who knows they're getting a real Christmas. Do you want to tell me what's going on?"

Cara's toes curled inside her too-small shoes. She didn't want to tell Betty, but she couldn't hide anything from the sharp-eyed old lady. "Well... I think I might be going to the feast this year," she admitted.

Betty's shoulders stiffened. "What makes you think that?" she asked.

Cara shot a desperate glance at Levi. "I think Mama might notice me," she said, "and ask me to come."

Betty snorted. "It would take a miracle," she said.

A thread of hope shot through Cara, brightest gold and burning hot. She grinned up at Betty, excitement throbbing in her chest. "It's Christmas, Betty," she said. "It's a good time for miracles, isn't it?"

Her eyes still on the turkey, Betty's voice grew soft. "I think sometimes we forget what miracles we already have," she murmured.

"What does that mean?" asked Cara.

"It means you're dreaming, Cara." Betty looked up at her, her eyes hard. "You're not going back up to that feast – this Christmas or any other. Make the best of what you've got and be content with it, that's what I always say. None of this fool-ishness about Christmas miracles."

Betty stamped off to the sink to wash her hands, and Cara glanced over at Levi, who gave her an encouraging smile. Betty had to be wrong – she just had to. Cara knew that it was high time she could get a miracle of her own.

And if there was any time that could be high time for a miracle, it had to be Christmas.

CHAPTER 10

A FEW HOURS LATER, Levi went out to get ready for dinner. The turkey left a little later, trussed, roasted, stuffed and drizzled in sauce. Christmas Eve slipped by.

And no one ever called for Cara.

The night had grown very long, the embers of the great log in the hearth burning down slowly to ashes, and still Cara couldn't bring herself to get up from the kitchen door where she'd been sitting ever since the turkey had gone out to the table. Waiters had come and gone through the door constantly, but now even they had retired to their own Christmas meal and left the kitchen. Betty had tried to get Cara to come with her to dinner, but Cara wouldn't move. She'd kept on hoping that any moment now Mama would remember her and send for her, and that she'd go up to the dining hall with its evergreen decorations and its bright-colored baubles.

But that time never came, and now even the dirty plates of Christmas dinner had come back inside. Cara could hear the scullery-maids hurrying to clean them down in the scullery. Betty had returned from her own dinner and was moving around in the kitchen, but she didn't try to say anything to Cara.

Cara was grateful for it. She thought that if someone spoke to her right now, she might open her mouth and scream and scream and scream. She could feel the sorrow and disappointment building up in a great, thick layer around her heart, as if her heart was being encrusted in lead.

Betty had been right all along. Mama didn't want her and never would. She'd always just be nothing, no one, the girl who slept on the floor, and nobody would ever like her except Levi and Betty.

She sniffed, trying to hold back her tears, but it was no use. Another Christmas was slipping past her without a feast or presents or family.

"Cara?"

Cara curled herself instinctively into the cold wall, turning her face away. "Go away," she whispered.

"I'm sorry about your Christmas, love." It was Betty, and her tone was as gruff as ever, but Cara thought she could feel real warmth somewhere beneath it. "I... have something for you."

Cara looked up. Betty was holding out one of her gnarled, calloused hands. "Come with me," she said.

It was a little surprising to take Betty's hard hand; Betty hadn't led her by the hand since she was very small. Still, it felt good, and Cara walked quietly beside her to the kitchen table. A little gasp escaped her.

There was no feast on the table, but there were a few little twigs from the pine trees outside, and even some leaves and berries from the holly bush by the table. They were all arranged around one of the servants' plates, where there rested a slice of some fine white meat, a blob of stuffing, and a little curl of sauce. There was also a slice of something that looked very much like plum pudding.

"B-Betty," Cara stammered.

Betty pulled out the chair. "It's not the Christmas feast you were hoping for," she said. "But I figured, well, those stuck-up folks won't even know about a bit o' their feast going missing. It's stealin', I suppose, but I just want to see a smile on that little face again."

Cara wished she could smile for Betty as she picked up the knife and fork and took her first bite of the plum pudding she'd made so many times before. Her nose was plugged from stifling her tears, and she could taste little other than their salty sorrow on her tongue, but she didn't have to taste it to know its sweetness. All the sweetness lay in the gentle eyes of Betty as she sat opposite her, watching her eat, her eyes filled with love and worry.

It was the bitterest and yet sweetest Christmas that Cara had ever known. Yet there was still a gaping hole, a great depth of longing in her heart, that no amount of Betty's kindness ever seemed to fill.

❧

THE DINING HALL'S candlelight was so brilliant that Cara could hardly bear to look at it. Holding a hand over her stinging eyes, Cara stepped out onto the shining, polished floor, feeling a gasp of awe lift her chest as she gazed around. The Christmas tree towered over one corner, all aglow with baubles and bright holly, hung with oranges and candy canes; stockings over the mantelpiece were in the brightest colours; on the table, Christmas crackers lay in neat rows. There was a huge pile of shining presents under the tree, wrapped in brown paper and pretty ribbons. Rows of cards stood on the mantelpiece over the stockings, each bearing some loving inscription. Cara ran to the mantelpiece, lifting a card. The paper was thick and sturdy; the image on the front showed a grinning Father Christmas clutching the reins of gentle-eyed reindeer.

Cara laughed with delight. She wasn't sure who this card was from, but she was excited for Mama to read it to her. Spinning around, she cried, "Mama."

The word echoed back at her from every shining corner. A strange feeling curled in Cara's gut; something that was an ugly hybrid of fear and disappointment. She backed away a little, looking wildly around the great hall.

"Mama?" she called again. "Levi?"

But there was no one. The enormous hall was utterly empty; Cara was the only living thing inside it. She ran to the table, but the chairs were all empty. Then to the door that led up to the staircase; she tugged at it, but it was locked.

"Mama! Glen!" she screamed. "I'm locked in." She yanked at the door again, its deafening rattle filling her world, but it wouldn't give. Slamming her hands against it, she heard her own voice rise to a sob. "Don't leave me here." she howled. "Levi! Betty! Someone!"

The door was still thundering as she yanked at it, and suddenly, there was a great bang from the lock.

Cara opened her eyes and sat up, gasping. The gilded hall with its pretty decorations was all gone. There was just the cold, dark kitchen, and the rattling was coming from the kitchen door as the cold winter wind rattled it on its hinges, sending a bitter draft underneath the door to curl around Cara's arms where she sat on her mat. Goosebumps rose on them, and she pulled her blanket up to her shoulders.

Of course. It was Christmas Eve – or probably Christmas morning, very early, by now – and Cara was all alone. Her family didn't want her.

Her family had never wanted her.

She huddled down in her blanket, closing her eyes, trying to find some sleep again before the hard work that awaited her on Christmas Day itself, but the ache of her heart wouldn't allow her to sleep. Why had Mama thrown her away – not just Mama Edna, but the one before that, too? And worse, why had Levi lied to her? Levi had been so sure that Mama would summon her this time. He'd made *her* feel so sure, and Levi was the only family she had.

Family. Cara wondered what that felt like, to be a part of a real family. Not something that could just be tossed aside, but a cherished child who belonged to someone. She was grateful to Betty's kindness, but she also knew that Betty would never have chosen to have her.

She'd thought that Mama had decided to have her as a daughter, yet she seemed to regret her choice. Levi had always treated her as a friend – but now even he had lied to her.

The kitchen had never felt so dark and empty. Cara closed her throbbing eyes, trying to remember a time that she truly belonged. Her heart brought her to a time that she could barely remember. The impression was vague and fuzzy; she knew she was very small, and that she was in a kitchen very much like this one. She was singing a song – or perhaps she was humming it – and a wispy figure in a maid's uniform bent over her.

My little hummingbird. The voice had been sweet, yet tired, and when the woman bent down, her eyes were dark and sad. She held out her arms, and Cara clambered into them, gripping the greasy locks of the woman's hair. *Mama,* she'd been saying. *Mama.*

Cara opened her eyes, looking at the dark kitchen once more. It was a strange memory, a simple one, but every time she was truly heartbroken, it kept on coming back to her. She'd tried not to think about it, since Mama Edna had told her that her first mother hadn't wanted her. But when she thought of the woman's soft eyes in her memory, she could almost believe that her first mama really had wanted her. That maybe Mama Edna hadn't been telling the truth.

Mama Edna had never really told her the truth.

Cara sat up, pushing her blanket away, her veins throbbing with this revelation. Maybe there *was* a family out there in the world, waiting for her – a real mama who wanted her. She only had one vague memory of her mother, but it was so vivid that she knew she'd recognize that face anywhere in all of London.

Cara got up, wrapping her only coat around her shoulders, and headed for the bread bin. If Mama, her real mama, was out there somewhere, then she'd have to find her.

With her real mama would be the only place she'd ever belong.

CHAPTER 11

CHRISTMAS EVE WAS NORMALLY one of Levi's favorite times of the year. The feast with all of its glorious delicacies – not only turkey and plum pudding, but also beef rib, mince pies, Yorkshire puddings, and sweetly sticky Christmas cake – was always a reminder of how much his life had changed since Papa had come to get him from the workhouse.

It had been hard to call him *Papa* at first. Levi had never known his real papa; he'd only ever known his big sister, and she'd died in that workhouse, leaving him to find a way to survive almost on his own among the crowds of little boys watched over by overwhelmed matrons. When Papa had rescued him five Christmases ago, he'd been just another suspicious stranger, someone who might turn on him at any moment. He'd only called him Papa because Mama had said he must, and Levi had figured that the only way to avoid a return to the workhouse was to behave exactly as the Halls wanted him to.

Now, *Mama* and *Papa* rolled off his tongue with ease. He'd said those names over and over again when he'd earnestly begged Mama to let Cara come to the Christmas feast, and he'd thought that his efforts were successful. Yet all through Christmas dinner, he'd kept his eyes on Mama, and she'd never once shown a sign that she even remembered the existence of the little girl she'd adopted.

It was as if Mama had only one child, and that was Levi. As if Cara didn't exist at all.

It had made him angry, but he knew better than to make a scene out of it during the feast, with the aunts and uncles and grandparents all around. Levi knew that to make a scene would be unforgivable, and then he'd never talk Mama into bringing Cara back into the home again.

So he'd gritted his teeth and smiled and laughed all through Christmas Eve, and only let out his angry tears when he'd gone to bed and sobbed into his silken pillow. Sleep had found him late that night, yet his guilt and shame woke him as soon as sunlight began to glimmer through the curtains of the great window in his room.

He pushed back his sheets at once, finding his slippers and warm gown. Everyone else would still be fast asleep – the adults had all still been up while he'd been tossing and turning. Everyone except the kitchen staff, ready to bring break-fast to Mama and Papa in bed.

Slipping out of the door, Levi padded down the hall as quietly as he could, desperate not to wake his parents or any of their overnight guests. He hurried down the stairs, then through the dining hall, which had already been cleaned and cleared up of last night's mess, left spotless despite the long and messy party the night before. The staff had already been up to clean it all this morning. His stomach clenched. Cara must have been among them, picking up the torn and crumpled wrapping paper, weeping over the fact that she never got the gifts that Levi had promised her. He had to make this up to her somehow.

When he stepped into the kitchen, he expected her to be on her mat, silent and angry. Instead, the kitchen was bustling madly with breakfast preparations. Maids were scampering every which way, their black-and-white uniforms flashing; Betty was at the kitchen table, chopping madly, and Cara's mat was empty.

Levi's heart sank. She wasn't here. Maybe she'd gone down to the stables; she liked to sit in the loft if she needed to be alone. He was turning to go when Betty's voice sailed through the chaos towards him.

"Levi. Thank goodness."

Something in her tone made fear leap in Levi's gut. He turned, his heart hammering in his chest. "Good morning,

Betty," he said, fighting through the crush of people to reach her elbow. She was cutting an onion with fierce efficiency; her eyes were dry. "Where's Cara?" Levi asked.

"What do you mean, where's Cara?" Betty stopped cutting suddenly, looking up at him, her knife poised above the chopping board.

"Well... I thought you might know," said Levi, bewildered. "She's not in the kitchen, is she?"

"No," said Betty. "I thought she was with you. That was why I was so glad to see you."

Levi tried to ignore the racing of his heart. "She must be in the stables."

"I already looked there. I already looked everywhere." Betty put down the knife with a rattle; her hands were shaking. "She's not upstairs?"

"No. Not at all. I would have known," said Levi.

Betty's face was always pallid, but now its colour grew even paler with fear. "She's run off," she said. "All your talk of miracles got her hopes up, boy, and now she's gone and run off with a broken little heart." She slammed a flat hand down on the table, more scared than angry. "Why did you have to go and do that to her?"

Levi felt tears burn his eyes. He knew that Betty was right, that she had every cause to be angry with him. "I'll find her," he said. "I'll find her. I have to tell Mama."

He ran out of the kitchen, heading upstairs as fast as his feet could carry him, not caring who heard his running footsteps. He had to find Cara.

He couldn't lose his only real friend.

IT WAS a little warmer now than it had been when Cara had first slipped out of the kitchen and into the street, but even so, her hands and feet had gone completely numb. The burning cold that she'd felt before had been painful, yet the numbness was worse. At least when her hands and feet had been hurting, she'd known that they still worked.

Tucking her fingers a little deeper under her armpits, Cara shivered, standing on a street corner as she looked up and down the road, trying to decide which way to go. The watery sunlight that struggled through a veil of dark clouds did little to warm her up, and even less to light her way. The morning was wearing on, yet there were street lamps still burning, their faded yellow glow looking strange and ghostly in the pale light. And the streets were quiet; eerily quiet. Cara had been out to town with Betty before on market days, and then the streets had been so full that it was nearly impossible to move, with carriages rushing up and down and a crush of people on the sidewalks.

Now, there was nearly nothing. Just Cara, and a gilded carriage trotting smartly down the street all alone, and a group of carollers going from one door to the next. They carried candles, their hands cupped around the flames to protect them from the frigid wind, and sang old songs in perfect, high voices. It would have been beautiful if Cara wasn't so cold and afraid.

She crossed the empty street, ignoring the holly wreaths on every doorway, and stumbled over to the carollers. They had stopped outside the door of a tall, thin house, and their gentle voices filled the air like candlelight. "Hark, the herald angels sing," they sang, led by a young woman with wonderful red-gold hair. "'Glory to the new-born King. Peace on earth, and mercy mild, God and sinners reconciled.'"

Peace on earth. Any kind of peace felt a long, long way away now, with Cara's hands freezing. She waited until the carollers finished their song and a woman had appeared at the door with pennies for all of them. Once the woman had closed the door, she stepped forward.

"Excuse me?" she whispered.

The girl with the red hair turned, a smile lifting her cheeks. "Oh, look at you." she said. "You poor little waif. Don't you have anywhere to go that's warmer than being out here?"

"No," said Cara, although it wasn't quite true; she could go back to the kitchen, she supposed, yet her heart drew her further on her mission. "I just want to find my mama."

"Where did you last see her?" asked one of the boys.

"I don't know. It was a long time ago," said Cara. "I wonder if you've seen her."

"What does she look like?" asked the red-haired girl.

"She's thin, and very white," said Cara, "and very pretty. Her eyes are big and dark, and she has mouse-brown hair." She touched her own. "She's a maid, or at least, she was a maid. I don't know anymore. Her name is Vickey." It had taken some concentrated effort to remember that much. "Vickey Cooper," she added, hazarding a guess. She remembered being called Cara Cooper herself; maybe her mysterious mother shared her name, at least.

"Vickey Cooper," said the redhead. "I'm sorry. I don't think..."

"Oi!" The yell came from across the street. "What are you doin', talking to that urchin?"

The redhead drew back, the rest of the young carollers huddling behind her. A huge, burly man, carrying a walking stick like a weapon, came striding toward them from across the street. He had a very red nose and two small, piggy black eyes that glittered malevolently down at Cara. "You're meant to be working." he bellowed at the children, who all recoiled, their candle flames guttering in protest at the sudden movement. He turned on Cara. "Get lost, waif," he barked, kicking up a spray of mud against her.

Cara gasped with cold and shock. She took a staggering step back. "I was only..."

"Go away," roared the man and swung his walking stick. It smacked into Cara's shoulder, sending a burst of pain blooming through her flesh. She rushed back, tripped, and landed on her bottom, clutching her aching shoulder, terrified and hurt. "GO!" he was yelling again, the stick raised in threat.

Cara didn't need to be told twice. She scrambled to her feet and bolted, clutching her shoulder, feeling warm tears splash on her feet—unable to understand why this cold world hated her so much on a Christmas morning like this one.

❧

LEVI FELT that he might explode.

He clutched his cup of Christmas coffee – a wonderful blend of whipped cream, chocolate, coffee and milk – without the usual relish as he watched Mama take a long sip from her own delicate mug. Propped up on her pillows, she was a little pale this morning, her eyes redder than usual. A little too much of that rum punch, Levi thought angrily.

It had been nearly a quarter of an hour since he'd burst into their bedroom, waking them both, much to Mama's disgust. She didn't want to hear a word of what he was saying about Cara's disappearance; in fact, she seemed almost ready to send him back to bed when Papa had tactfully intervened and told Levi to send for a maid and get some morning coffee. Now, Levi sat on the foot of the bed, almost dancing with impatience as Mama took another leisurely sip. Didn't she care at all about Cara? Had she never cared at all?

At last, Mama lowered her cup to its saucer and gave Levi a calm look. "Now, my boy," she said, "tell us what's made you forget all of your manners this morning."

Levi's hand trembled on his own cup, nearly spilling on the lovely sheets. "Cara's gone," he burst out.

Mama's cup rattled in its saucer, but her shock was momentary. When she looked at Levi over the rim of her steaming cup, her face was calm, yet Levi saw something flash in her eyes. It wasn't concern. With a dreadful lurch in his belly, he realized that it was anger.

It was Papa who spoke. "Gone?" he said, putting aside his own cup and saucer. "What do you mean, she's gone?"

"She's disappeared, Papa," said Levi, relieved. Often, when it came to Cara, Papa simply seemed to follow Mama's lead. "She was here last night and now she's disappeared."

"Oh, I'm sure she's around here somewhere," said Mama, waving an elegant, dismissive hand.

"Maybe she's just hiding somewhere," Papa suggested. "I think we should ask Betty."

"Who's Betty?" said Mama.

"The cook," said Papa. There was a remonstrance in his voice. "She's been caring for Cara, darling." His eyes met Levi's, and Levi realized that talking to Mama was useless when it came to Cara. The only flicker of caring he could find was in his adoptive father's eyes.

"I've already spoken to Betty," said Levi. "She's been searching all morning – she can't find her either."

"What were you doing in the kitchens this morning, Levi?" Mama demanded, her eyes flashing.

"I was looking for Cara." Levi heard his voice rise and struggled to control it again.

"You hang about with that girl too much," said Mama.

"Edna." Papa's tone was gentle, but there was a strength beneath it. "You adopted Cara, remember? Just like we adopted Levi. You can't throw her aside like this – she's practically his sister."

Levi couldn't understand the look in Mama's eyes. There was rage there, but something else: shame. He struggled to grasp where it had come from. "I just want to find her," he said, exhausted by his mother's complex emotions. "I just want to bring her back."

"She'll come back when she's hungry. In the meantime, don't ruin Christmas with this, Levi," said Mama. "We're going to have a lovely time today – a nice breakfast, then church, and..."

"I don't think I can do that while Cara's missing, Mama," said Levi. "What if she's in trouble?"

"I'm sure she's just run off, stupid child," said Mama. "As for you, Levi, you're becoming very impudent. Unless you want to spend Christmas locked in the nursery, I suggest you put that girl out of your head and listen to your elders and betters."

Levi lowered his head, feeling the hot sting of tears behind his eyes. "Yes, Mama," he whispered.

"Now go to your room and get yourself dressed," said Mama sharply. "I don't want to hear any more from you."

Levi sighed, slipping off the bed, and slumped toward the door. Before he could close it behind him, however, Papa was beside him, his bare feet padding on the carpet. He was shrugging on his robe, calling over his shoulder, "I'll be right back, darling." But as soon as the door was closed, Papa closed his big, warm hand over Levi's.

"Give me a few minutes," he said. "I'll convince her. You and I will go out and search for Cara right away – don't you worry."

"Oh, Papa." Levi clutched his hand. "Thank you."

"We can't let the poor little thing stay out there all night. She'll freeze to death." Papa shuddered. "Now get dressed warmly – and leave your mother to me."

CHAPTER 12

CARA'S EYES felt hot and tired from all the crying. Her feet ached, and her hands were numb with cold as she stumbled through the twilit streets, going from one glowing streetlamp to the other. All the windows were golden with candlelight; she could just imagine the families behind them, sitting down to another lavish meal, or perhaps just leftovers from Christmas dinner. There would be warmth and laughter, and the smell of roasting chestnuts, and presents. All the things that Cara had ever wanted for Christmas. She had believed so hard that she'd be getting all those things this year, yet it had been just the same. She was irrevocably separated from Christmas itself by the cold hard width of a pane of glass.

Not even Mama seemed to be anywhere on these streets, and as the day had worn on, Cara had begun to realize just how many streets there were in London. They seemed to go on forever and ever. Every time she turned a corner, hoping to see the house she vaguely remembered, there was just another alien street before her. Houses she didn't know. Squares she'd never seen before.

She had no idea that the world could be so big, and with every mile her small feet trod, she was starting to believe that it was much too big for her to find one single woman in it.

Perhaps it would have been easier if even one of the people she passed would have tried to help her. She'd been so sure, that morning, that the miracle spirit of Christmas would be in their hearts. Hadn't they been singing about it for weeks? Goodwill, peace, mercy, love – wasn't that what Christmas was supposed to be? But when Cara looked into the eyes of the men and women on the streets, she saw only cold and hardness. She had asked all day, and no one wanted to help her.

The last person she asked was an old gentleman with red cheeks and twinkling eyes, who practically rolled out of his carriage in front of a pretty cottage, talking jovially to his companions. He seemed so much like the Father Christmas she'd seen on the card in her dream that she couldn't help thinking that he'd at least smile at her, even if he couldn't help her.

"Excuse me, sir?" she'd said, stepping forward. "I'm looking for my mama, and..."

The jolly old gentleman moved faster than Cara would have thought possible. His elbow lashed out, slamming into her cheekbone with crunching force. She stumbled back, landing heavily on the sidewalk, half blind with pain. Tears sprang to her eyes as she raised a hand to her throbbing cheekbone.

The old gentleman spat an expletive at her. "Get away with you, foul little urchin." he growled, and he and his companions all swaggered into their cottage, slamming the door behind them.

Now it was growing very dark, and Cara had long since given up on asking anyone for help. In fact, she thought she was starting to give up on finding Mama at all; at least, for tonight. She was starting, instead, to think about the cold that came creeping out of the shadows. The streets lay slumbering beneath a coat of white snow that had always looked so lovely from the kitchen windows. In reality, now that she was among it, it wasn't lovely at all. It was brutal. Her hands and feet ached with it, and hunger made her grow tired. She'd finished the heel of bread she'd taken from the kitchen the night before.

She felt her eyes fill with tears as she stumbled along the streets, nearly too tired to move, yet driven by the knowledge that to stop now would be to freeze to death. Oh, for that warm kitchen, for her mat by the fire, for a hearty meal from Betty. But what use was it? The kitchen was comfortable, but no one wanted her there. Betty cared for her but would never have chosen her. And Levi...

A sob lifted her chest, and Cara watched a glistening tear bounce off her coat and splatter on the sidewalk. She'd thought that Levi wanted her, but he'd lied to her. He'd made a promise he couldn't keep, and where was he now? Nowhere. There was just Cara, alone in this massive world, with the winter cold coming ever nearer as the darkness intensified.

When her legs grew too weary to move, Cara stumbled into an alleyway, where at least the ramshackle walls shielded her from the wind. Even out of the wind, the cold felt like a living thing with razor-edged fangs of ice that sank deep into her flesh. There was a figure huddled at the end of the alley; Cara stared at it in fear for a few long moments until she saw that the tramp was fast asleep, his mouth hanging open, a snore whistling between the gap where his front teeth should be.

He seemed harmless enough, and she was too tired to go on. She crept towards a wooden box that lay on its side, one of its slats broken, letting in a thin layer of snow. Sweeping it out with her numb hands, she slipped into it, curling herself within the box's hard corners. She wasn't sure that it was any real shelter from the cold, but at least it felt like shelter from the world.

Cramming her frozen fists under her chin, she closed her eyes and gave herself over to sheer exhaustion.

"Cara?"

The voice was the only thing in the darkness. It twisted through the silence, something silver and bright in a world that was nothing but a great, cold, black voice. Cara listened to it, wondering where she'd heard it before. There was a part of her that knew she should know, yet she was so comfortable. Thinking, let alone moving, felt like too much effort.

"Cara," the voice called again.

It was a nice voice; Cara wasn't sure why it made her heart hurt. She sighed, then regretted it, the extra lift of her ribcage sending a pang of pain down the length of her body.

"Papa," the voice was gasping. "Look – in the box. Is that... is that her?"

Another voice joined it, deeper, and frightened. "Stay back, Levi."

"But Papa..."

"I said, stay back."

Cara groaned. She wished the voices would just go away. They were nice, but she wanted to sleep, to give herself over to that numb darkness.

Then, warmth. Something was touching her arm, gripping it, dragging her forward. Her stiff joints stabbed with pain in protest. "Cara!" the second voice cried. The hand on her arm gave her a shake, and it made her muscles sting. "Wake up."

Cara groaned with pain.

"Oh, thank goodness." The second voice... *Glen*. It was Mama's husband, Glen. He sounded relieved, almost tired. "She's alive."

"Cara!" the first voice gasped again, and this time, she recognized it; it was Levi. Her eyes snapped open, and she was looking at the alley, bathed in the wobbling light from the lantern that swung from Levi's hand. The angle of the lantern made his features look sharper, casting black, edged shadows under his eyes and nose. She blinked up at him, aware that her joints were all stiff and sore with cold, but mostly surprised to see him.

"Levi?" she whispered.

"You're so cold," Glen murmured. He was pulling off his coat, bundling it around her, sitting her up against the wall of the alley. "What were you thinking, child?"

Cara stared at him, but he seemed more scared than angry, so she looked back up at Levi. "What are you doing here?" she asked.

There was no rage in Levi's face, just regret, welling up in his eyes like tears. He set the lantern down and knelt beside her. "We're looking for you, of course."

"You came looking for me?" Cara murmured.

She saw Glen flinch at the words, but Levi's reaction was greater. This time, his eyes really were filling with tears. "Of course, I did," said Levi. "Did you think I wouldn't notice that you were gone?"

That had been exactly what Cara feared, but now he was here, in the pitch darkness on the night of Christmas. He must have told Glen that she was gone.

"We've been searching for you all day," Levi added. "What happened? Why did you run away?"

"I thought you didn't want me anymore," whispered Cara.

Glen was chafing her small hands between his own, and she relished the feeling of warmth returning to them. Levi didn't look at her; his eyes were on the dirt at his feet, but he reached out and put his hand on her shoulder.

"I'll always want you, Cara," he whispered.

And that was the first time that Cara felt the warm spark of Christmas spirit in her heart.

CHAPTER 13

EVEN THOUGH THE Christmas decorations in the hall were brilliantly gaudy, Glen's heart felt cold and grey on the inside as he stepped over the threshold, allowing the butler to help him out of his thick coat. It had been a long, freezing day searching the streets for that poor little girl. He'd been genuinely afraid that she was dead when he and Levi had stumbled upon her curled up in that wooden box; her hands and legs had been very blue, and there had been frost on her eyelashcs.

Now, at least, Cara was safely back in the kitchen, bundled in a blanket and sipping soup as Betty clucked over her. She was safely home – but not where she belonged, Glen thought. He still couldn't understand why Edna had so suddenly rejected the child that she'd brought home five Christmases ago.

Maybe getting Levi from the workhouse had been a mistake, Glen thought, watching as the boy thanked the butler for taking his own coat and then carefully stepped out of his wet, cold shoes. The thought was like a hot poker in his heart. He couldn't think like that. Levi was the best thing Glen had ever done, one of the few decisions he never regretted. As if feeling his father's gaze on him, Levi looked up, his deep brown eyes smiling. He reached over and wrapped his small hand in Glen's.

"Thank you, Papa," he said. "Thank you for going to find Cara."

"Of course, my boy." Glen held out his arms. "Come here."

He drew Levi into his embrace, even though he knew it was unfashionable, and kissed the top of the boy's tousled head. It was hard to remember, sometimes, that Levi wasn't his biological son. He was certainly the one thing that Glen treasured the most.

Footsteps rang on the winged staircase, and Glen stepped back, letting go of Levi. He felt his stomach clench as he looked up. Edna was waiting imperiously at the top of the stairs, her fur robe wrapped around herself, hair piled neatly on top of her head and aglitter with jewel-studded pins.

"You're back," she said.

"Mama!" Levi's face lit up, and he ran to her, arms extended. "We found her, Mama. She's safe. She's back in the kitchen, safe and sound."

"I told you she was all right," sniffed Edna, giving Levi a half-hearted embrace. "The stupid little girl had just run off."

Mounting the steps himself, Glen cut in. "Levi, why don't you run along and wash up?" he said. "I'm sure you're hungry, but you can't go to dinner all dirty." Reaching them, he ran a hand through the boy's hair.

"All right. Thanks, Papa," said Levi. He pelted off down the corridor, looking like a ten-year-old boy for the first time all day.

Glen watched him go, smiling. When Edna stepped into his vision, it felt like an imposition.

"I hope you know what you've done to me." Raising her nose into the air, Edna pulled her robe around her shoulders. "I had to receive all of our Christmas guests alone. I don't know how I managed it. You utterly ruined the whole thing for me, Glen. I don't know how you could be so selfish."

Staring at her, Glen wondered what had happened to his sweet, doting wife. Nothing had been the same since... well, since Cara had come to their home.

"Come now, Edna." Glen reached for her hand, wrapping it in his own even though his fingers were cold from the long search in the dark. "We couldn't have just left the poor child to fend for herself. She wasn't all right, you know – the poor little mite was half dead when we reached her."

"I knew it." Edna turned away, pulling her hand out of his own. "You love her more than you love me."

"Edna…" Glen reached for her shoulder instead. "I would have left Cara to go looking for you, if you were in danger. You know that. I would have moved heaven and earth to search for you."

"You don't understand, Glen," Edna cried, looking up at him with eyes that swam with tears. "That little Cara has been nothing but trouble ever since she first came here. She's demanded attention, she's caused chaos in the household, and now she's causing a quarrel between the two of us. How could you love her more than you love me?"

"I love you more than breath," said Glen softly. "And I also love our children. *Both* of our children."

Edna had gone very quiet. She glared at Glen, frozen like a lovely statue, no less beautiful than she'd been on her wedding day despite the streaks of silver that glowed among her blonde curls where they tumbled softly over her bare, milk-pure shoulders.

"We have to care for Cara just as we do for Levi," said Glen gently. "I have been painfully remiss, and I regret it."

"We don't have to care for her like Levi," snapped Edna.

"Why not?"

"Because I *want* Levi," said Edna. "I've regretted Cara ever since the day I took her."

Glen stepped back, letting his hand fall to his side. "What do you mean... *took* her?" he said slowly.

Edna's eyes widened, and fear glowed in them for a moment that made Glen's stomach turn over. Then she pressed the back of her hand to her forehead, letting out a sob.

"Oh, my head." she cried. "It's so painful. She's ruined Christmas, Glen, she's utterly ruined it. I'm going straight to bed."

She swept away, her robe billowing around her, leaving Glen to stare after her with a terrible suspicion in the pit of his stomach. Maybe his wife had just meant that she'd taken Cara from the workhouse.

But he knew that nothing had been the same since Cara had come to live with them. That Edna had been acting strangely for the past five years. And he couldn't stop the fear from rising slowly in his heart.

Betty welcomed Cara back with an uncharacteristic show of tears, wrapping her so tightly in her stout arms and cuddling her so close to her chest that it frightened Cara. Had running away really been so dangerous? Yet, as Betty held her close and sobbed into her hair, Cara thought of how she'd felt when Glen and Levi had woken her. A jolt of fear ran through her. She knew she'd nearly frozen to death out there.

Betty's sobs quickly turned to scolding. "You naughty, naughty, naughty little girl." she gasped, still clinging to Cara and crying into her hair. "How could you do this to your Betty?"

"I'm sorry, Betty," said Cara, meaning it. She could feel her own eyes filling with tears of regret. "I didn't mean to do anything wrong. I didn't mean to frighten you."

"Land's sakes, child, how did you think I would feel coming to the kitchen during Christmas time to see you'd vanished?" Betty demanded. She pulled back to glare at Cara, her eyes swimming with tears. "I thought I'd lost you."

"I'm sorry," said Cara again.

"Why, I'd be out there myself if Glen and Levi hadn't gone to look for you." She pushed Cara down onto her mat and wrapped her in a blanket – a good thick one she'd taken from her own bed. "Thank goodness they found you. You would have frozen, you silly little mite."

Cara accepted the bowl of soup that was thrust into her hands. It was hot and salty and savoury and very, very good. She scalded her mouth on the first spoonful, then blew on the second. "I was just looking for my mama," she said. "My first mama."

Betty sighed. "I know you were disappointed about Christmas, dear," she said. "But don't you go doing such a silly thing ever again, do you hear me?" Her hands were shaking as she grasped Cara's shoulders and planted a kiss on the top of her head. "There are people who care for you here. Don't forget it."

After the soup, Cara lay wrapped in her blanket, thinking about Betty's words after the cook had put a last log on the fire and retired to her own quarters. She watched the dance of the flames. After Christmas dinner had come and gone without Cara being summoned to the table, she'd thought that there was no one here left to care about her. But Levi and Glen had come looking for her – and Betty had been so happy about her return, she'd cried.

Betty was right. There were people here who loved Cara, and she couldn't understand why that fact wasn't enough for her aching young heart.

Her swirl of confused thoughts couldn't stand up to the exhaustion seeping into her mind, and in a matter of minutes, she was fast asleep.

CHAPTER 14

Once again, it was a voice and a gentle touch that woke her as Levi laid a hand on her shoulder. "Cara?"

She blinked at him, her eyes feeling hot and fuzzy with sleep. He held a candlestick in one hand, the little yellow flame sputtering as he moved; his nightshirt hung down to his knees under a furry robe, and his sleeping cap was askew on his messy hair.

Sitting up, Cara rubbed her eyes. "Levi? What time is it? It must be so late."

"Actually, it's very early – about four o' clock in the morning on Boxing Day," said Levi.

"What are you doing down here?" Cara yawned.

"Something I should have done a long time ago." Levi held out a hand to her. "Come with me."

She stared at him, and her heart could find no reason to say no. Reaching out, she let him wrap her cold little fingers in his warm hand.

"Where are we going?" she asked.

"It's a secret." Levi grinned at her, his eyes sparkling.

Cara giggled as he led her to the kitchen door, and he laid a finger to his lips, his shush fragmented by little wobbles of laughter. "Quiet," he said. "We don't want to wake Mama and Papa."

Papa. Cara hadn't spoken to Glen often enough to call him that, but she was starting to feel like he was the closest thing she'd ever had to a father, now that he'd come to find her. "I was so glad when you and... and Papa came to find me," she whispered.

"Of course, we did," said Levi. "We love you, Cara."

He said it simply, as if it was obvious, and Cara sighed with longing to be as close to Levi as they would have been if they were brother and sister.

Now, he was leading her on her cold, bare feet across the marble hall and up one of the majestic, winged staircases. She clutched the hem of her grubby dress in excitement; her hand was growing sweaty in his, but she refused to let go. "I haven't been upstairs in years," she whispered.

"And that's not right," said Levi. "It's your home too, you know."

"It doesn't feel that way," said Cara, sticking close to him as they walked down the long, carpeted hallway, their feet silent in the deep fabric. She'd never liked this hallway, which was lined with portraits of grumpy-looking old men and women that frowned down at her through lorgnettes and monocles. In the light of Levi's candle, they looked ghostly and pale, as if their vengeful spirits might plunge from the canvas at any moment and eat both the children alive.

"Well, I'm hoping to change that," said Levi gently.

He pushed open a doorway, and when Cara stepped inside, she realized it was the door of the nursery that had been her room for a few brief months. She was startled to see how much smaller everything was than the way she remembered it. In her mind, the bed had been the size of an entire room; the wardrobe that had always terrified her and had felt as tall as a tower, now it looked rather sad and ordinary. The dolls and girls' toys that had been strewn over the room were gone, replaced by a beautiful dapple-grey rocking horse in the corner, a row of tin soldiers on the dresser, and long rows of books in the shelves.

And in the middle of the room, a quilt lay spread out on the floor, a candle casting a golden light at its centre. There were sprigs of holly lying all around it, and a plate on each side. There was even something that looked rather like a home-made Christmas cracker, only it was made from brown paper instead of the bright colours of the crackers Cara had seen in the dining hall.

"Merry Christmas, Cara," said Levi softly.

"Oh." Cara clapped her hands to her mouth to muffle her own surprise as Levi closed the door and set his candle on a nook in the wall. She stepped forward. "Is this for me?"

"It is," said Levi. He shuffled his feet, looking sheepish. "I... well, it just felt so wrong to me that you're sleeping on a mat in the kitchen when I have a lovely room like this. I wanted you to have a nice Christmas like you should have had. I know it's really Boxing Day, but I hope it's not too late."

"It's lovely," said Cara. "I... I love it."

"I'm glad to hear it." Levi grinned. "Come – sit down. I stole these from the kitchen, but I suppose it's not really stealing since it belongs to my family."

It was every bit of the Christmas feast that Cara had helped to prepare, yet never been able to partake of. None of the food was as tasty as it had been when Betty had made it for her, but this Christmas feast had all of the trimmings: the crackers, the cards, and even a gift, all of them little things that Levi had made himself from bits of cardboard and brown paper. The cracker contained a silly paper hat and a few little pieces of chocolate; it had been years since Cara had had chocolate, and it melted gloriously in her mouth while Levi leaned over to adjust the paper hat on her head. He was wearing a cardboard crown himself, and it kept falling askew over one eye. Their giggles filled the little room, and they had to keep shushing one another.

The gift was even better. It was a little doll, not the hard porcelain kind, but a sweet soft thing with stringy golden hair and a big smile embroidered on the round face. Cara gasped as she lifted it from the wrapping. "Where did you get this?" she cried, cuddling it.

"I think Mama bought it for you years ago," said Levi. "I found it under my bed not long after you went to sleep in the kitchen, and I've been keeping it for you."

"I love her," Cara breathed, stroking the soft hair. "I love her forever and ever."

"Good," laughed Levi softly. "Now – why don't you read your card?"

Cara felt shame burn her cheeks. She lowered both the doll and her eyes. "I can't," she said.

"What do you mean?" asked Levi. He opened it and held it out to her, tipping it so that the candlelight flickered on the words he'd scratched into the paper. "I wrote it nice and big so that you can see it easily in the dark."

"I..." Cara looked away from him, clutching the doll. "I can't read."

"Oh." Levi hesitated a moment, staring at her, and Cara wished that the floor would open up and swallow her whole and whisk her away to another universe, one where she was worthy, where neither of her mothers had thrown her away and where she didn't have to sit in front of Levi in her rags. But the moment passed only a second before a smile split his face.

"That's all right." he said eagerly. "I'll read to you."

"Oh, please do." said Cara, shuffling closer.

His voice was as warm as the candlelight as he read. "Dear Cara, I wish Mama was nicer to you," he read. "Papa and I wish you could stay upstairs with us. We like you very much and we don't want you to run away again. Please stay with us. One day we'll give you a lovely Christmas. Love, Levi."

"Thank you," said Cara quietly. "I think maybe this is the best Christmas ever."

"Even though you nearly froze to death?" said Levi.

"Yes, even though," said Cara.

"How's that possible?" Levi asked.

Cara smiled at him. "Because you came to find me," she said.

"GOOD HEAVENS, CHILD," said Betty grumpily. "It's a good thing I have big feet, or you would have swallowed me."

"Sorry, Betty," Cara said, squeezing the words out through the tail end of a huge yawn. She rubbed her eyes, then turned her attention back to the potatoes she was peeling.

Betty gave an irritable grunt. "And cover your mouth when you yawn," she said. "Hurry up now, child. It's only January, but it'll be Christmas all over again by the time you've cut up those potatoes for the stew."

Cara blinked against the tiredness lurking at the corners of her eyes, but it was a good sort of tiredness, not the kind that made her feel heavy and lost. She smiled at the memory of the night before. It had been a few weeks since Christmas, but those few weeks had been lovely. Almost every night, Levi sneaked her up to his room, and they played on the floor while slants of streetlamp light danced on Levi's eyes and hair.

Letting out a happy sigh, she tossed the last of the potato peels into the compost bin and took out a kitchen knife to get started on cutting them. That was when she noticed Betty's eyes on her. The cook was watching her sharply, her hands still busy with the turnips she was chopping.

"What is it?" Cara asked nervously.

Betty put down her knife and folded her arms. "You tell me, Cara," she said. "I'm starting to think perhaps you didn't listen to what I told you about going upstairs."

Cara felt her cheeks grow warm. "You didn't say I couldn't go."

"No, I suppose I didn't," said Betty irritably. "But maybe I should have. No good can come of it, Cara."

"But I like going upstairs," said Cara. "Levi's so nice, and it's fun to have someone to play with. And he's teaching me to read and write, too. I really like learning. I can make most of the letters on his slate now."

"That's as may be," grunted Betty, "and perhaps it's not a bad thing you're learning to read and write – I would teach you if I had the patience. And I know you and Levi are good friends. It's unnatural, a little scrap like you without anyone to play with."

"So why are you angry with me?" asked Cara.

Betty sighed. "I'm not angry, Cara," she said. "I'm worried." She reached out, laying a hand on Cara's shoulder. "I don't want your little heart to be broken another time."

"What do you mean?" said Cara. "Levi wouldn't do anything to hurt me."

"I know *Levi* won't," said Betty. "But if Mrs. Hall finds out..."

Cara felt her stomach do a little somersault. She pictured what Mama would do if she knew that Cara was coming upstairs to the forbidden nursery every night. Would she chase Cara right out of the house? Where would she go then?

She'd have to find her real mama, Vickey, and even though her heart hurt to find her, she'd learned that looking for her was harder than she'd expected.

"She won't find out," she said, trying desperately to believe it. "Levi won't tell. And I haven't told anyone, except you. And you wouldn't tell, would you, dear Betty?"

"Of course not," said Betty. "But you mark my words, Cara, you two should stop meeting like that. Mrs. Hall *is* going to find out, some way or another – and if she does, you'll be in deep trouble."

Cara didn't know what to say. Part of her was terrified that Betty was right, and yet she couldn't bring herself to think of stopping. "I just love to play with Levi," said Cara softly. "He's so kind to me. Like you."

Betty sighed. "And that's why I don't forbid it," she said. She tossed the turnips into a tureen. "Come on now with those potatoes – we need to go over to the butcher's for a side of ham."

"You'll help me look for her, won't you?" said Cara, slicing the first potato in half, then into strips, then cubes.

Betty didn't have to ask. Every time she'd taken Cara out onto the streets to buy supplies, ever since Christmas, she'd had to make the same promise: to look out for a woman matching Cara's vague memory of her real mama.

"Of course, I will," she said.

Once the stew was boiling merrily on the stove, sending bursts of savoury aroma into the air, Cara pulled her coat around her shoulders, and Betty took her sturdy shopping basket from its place by the door.

"Can Dolly come?" Cara asked, grabbing the pretty golden-haired doll where it lay on the matt.

Betty gave a long look, then sighed, her shoulders sagging. "Oh, all right," she said. "If she must."

"Thank you." Cara tucked the dolly under her arm and allowed Betty to wrap her hand firmly in her big, calloused fingers, and they headed out into a bleak January day. Everything was grey and cold; the sketched lines of the trees' bare branches against the sky looked so much like a drawing that Cara felt she might smudge them if she reached out too quickly.

The rattle of carriage wheels reached them as they walked down the little path leading from the servants' entrance to the street. Cara peered through the pine trees separating the vegetable garden from the lawn to see a flash of gold. Mama was headed off somewhere in her gilded carriage, with Levi probably in tow. She smiled, knowing she'd hear all about it tonight when he came to get her.

"Have you ever ridden in a carriage, Betty?" she asked.

"Not a carriage, no," said Betty. "A cab, yes, a few times. But they cost the earth – and besides, walking keeps you warm, so let's go."

She pushed open the garden gate, and as Cara stepped out onto the sidewalk, a gust of wind came roaring icily down the street, hurling a prickling handful of cold sleet in her face. Cara gasped, raising a hand to shield her face, and the wind pounced on the doll she'd tucked under her arm, plucking it out.

"No!" Cara cried, grabbing frantically as the doll was swept into the air. "Dolly!"

"Cara!" Betty yelled, grabbing her arm as the sound of hoof-beats echoed down the street toward them.

Cara wasn't looking at the street or at the approaching carriage. She stared as the doll flopped out of the air, landing with a loud splat in the slushy gutter. The hoofbeats were almost upon them now – if the carriage would just pass them, then Cara could run and grab the poor little wct doll from the gutter...

"STOP!"

It was Mama's voice, and it shrieked horribly in the winter air. The coachman leaned back on the reins, and Mama's four white horses all but sat down on their haunches, their mouths wide in protest. The carriage skidded to a halt, and Mama's head appeared out of the window. Her cheeks were red with pleasant warmth, but her eyes burned with cold where they rested on Cara.

She extended an imperious finger out of the window. "Where did you get that?" she barked.

She was pointing at the doll. Wrenching her arm away from Betty, Cara ran to it and snatched the soggy object up, pressing it to her chest. She was gripped with a sudden fear that Mama would try to take it away from her.

"Where did you get it, child?" Mama repeated angrily.

Levi was sitting beside her, his face shadowed in the carriage's curtained interior, but Cara could see the glint of the whites of his eyes. He was terrified, just like her. Cara's breath caught in her chest, and she was losing herself in Mama's frigid eyes when a warm hand wrapped itself around her own and Betty's smooth voice slipped between them like a shield.

"Oh, don't mind her, ma'am," said Betty easily. "She brought it with her when she was moved down to the kitchen. It's needed some patchwork over the years, but it's all she has."

Her voice was silky-smooth, yet it held an iron sharpness in it that made Mama draw back into the warmth of the carriage. "Keep that child under control, Cook," she said imperiously. She leaned back in her velvet seat. "Get on with it, Patrick."

The coachman snapped the whip, and the carriage rumbled off again, but Cara couldn't forget the look in Mama's eyes.

It was more than just cold. It was hatred.

CHAPTER 15

IT WAS GETTING dark by the time the carriage made its way back toward home, and Levi leaned back in his seat, exhausted. He'd been on pins and needles ever since Mama had spotted the doll that the wind had plucked out of Cara's hands. She'd allowed them to drive on, but he wasn't sure if that was just because she didn't want to be late to another silly tea party with her friends; he knew she wanted to impress Mrs. Hampton, who had been bragging about how fast her husband's new horses were.

All the way to Mrs. Hampton's house, however, Mama had been quiet, and once they got there everything had seemed fairly normal. She'd sipped tea from her china cup and talked casually about expensive things in their house, and Levi had played quietly and politely on the carpet with Mrs. Hampton's four daughters. They were all very stuck-up, but he pretended to like them because Mama wanted him to. She called them "civilized company" even though none of them ever said "please" or "thank you" like Cara did.

Finally, they were on their way home now, with the coach-lamps swinging with the rhythm of the horses and sparkling on falling snow, and Mama hadn't said anything about Cara. Maybe she'd forgotten all about her. Levi leaned back, closing his eyes. Perhaps he could have a nap before they got home.

"Tired?" said Mama.

Levi opened his eyes and watched her warily. There was an edge in her voice that he didn't like.

"A little bit," said Levi.

"I'm not surprised." Mama turned her head away. "Considering it seems like you've hardly slept a wink in the past few weeks."

Levi felt his stomach clench. How much did she know? He didn't know what to say, so he stayed silent, listening to the racing rush of the blood in his ears.

"I sleep lightly, you know," she went on. "My head aches so ever since you and your father ruined Christmas for me." She reached up to press her delicate fingers into the bridge of her nose. "Some nights I wake up and hear you playing in your nursery."

"I... I have trouble sleeping sometimes, Mama," Levi stammered out.

Mama's voice cut like a stiletto. "I'm sure you do," she said, "considering the company that you keep."

Levi held his breath.

"I don't know why you insist on breaking your poor mother's heart so, Levi," said Mama. "I've given you everything, you know. You were just a poor little workhouse boy, and I've made you into a fine little gentleman. There's nothing you've ever had want of in my house. You're my own son to me, as much as if you were my son by blood, and I can't understand why you would betray me like this."

"Mama, I don't want to do anything to hurt you," said Levi. "I just feel sorry for Cara. She used to sleep in the nursery too, and..."

"Everything I do is for your sake, darling," said Mama, cutting him off abruptly. "That child is a bad influence on you. She makes you ungrateful and impudent. Look what she's done. She's convinced you to hide things from your own mother."

Levi hung his head, feeling a pang of shame. He'd never wanted to lie to Mama. But how was it fair that Cara had to sleep in the kitchen, and he in his lavish bedroom?

"It's not Cara's fault," he said softly. "It was all my idea. Please, if you're angry, be angry with me, not her."

Mama's eyes narrowed. "I shouldn't even allow that child in my house," she said. "I should send her back to the workhouse."

The threat ran down Levi's spine like a bolt of ice. The workhouse. His memories of it were fading on the whole, but some were brilliant in their painfulness. The way the other boys had kicked him, pushing him aside at mealtimes, left him to lick at their empty bowls for the sad, oily smears of the gruel they'd left behind. The mistress' sharp voice screaming at him during lessons when he failed to understand her instructions through the cacophony of the other boys' constant activity. And the day the matron had led him by the hand into a cold, dark room, where his dead sister lay in a paper-thin coffin, on her way to a pauper's mass grave...

He realized that tears were running down his cheeks, and he couldn't keep calm anymore. He grabbed Mama's hand in his own trembling fingers. "Mama, please," he begged. "Please, don't do that. Don't send Cara away. Don't let her go to that awful, awful place."

"That's in your hands, Levi," said Mama coldly. "Not my own."

He drew back. "What do you mean?"

"I mean that if you insist on playing with that girl, you'll leave me no choice," said Mama.

"You... you don't want me to be friends with her anymore?"

"I don't want you to *speak* to her anymore," said Mama. She turned to him, giving him the full force of a glare that twisted her face so that she was barely recognizable as his mother. "Or I *will* send her to the workhouse, Levi."

Levi felt his hands trembling. He closed his eyes, his impossible choice ripping at his heart.

"Please, Mama, don't," he whispered.

"I won't," said Mama sharply, "if you do as I say."

He leaned his forehead against the window of the carriage, surprised by the thump of his heart. It felt so broken that he could have sworn it had already stopped beating.

❧

THE BIG CLOCK on the kitchen wall said twenty minutes past eleven. Cara knew that because Levi had been teaching her, just last night, how to read the face of a clock; the little fat hand showed the hour, and the long thin hand showed the minutes. She knew that if the long hand pointed to the one it meant five minutes, and the two meant ten minutes, but she couldn't remember any of the rest – except twenty past eleven, because it had been exactly twenty past eleven when Levi had shown her how to read a clock last night.

He was late. Very late.

Mama and Glen normally went to bed right after ten, and Levi would be padding down the stairs to come and get Cara from the kitchen just before eleven, every single night. She knew that much because she could hear the chime of the church bells down the street. But now the minutes were slipping by, and she sat very still with her doll – which had been hung in front of the fire to dry – clutched tightly in her hands.

The church clock chimed the half-hour, and Cara tried not to think of all the reasons why Levi hadn't come to get her. She tried not to think that he didn't love her anymore or that something terrible had happened. She'd heard about accidents on the road before. But three plates had gone up to the table for each course of supper, and three empty plates had come back. That meant he had to be home.

He'd fallen asleep, she decided. They'd been at the tea party late, and he'd been tired and fallen asleep while he was waiting for his parents to wake up. It was a nice possibility, one that held no fear for her, so she snatched at it and held it close. Maybe she should just go to sleep and see him tomorrow.

But the nervousness in her gut wouldn't let her, she knew that much. Instead, perhaps she should creep up the stairs herself and surprise him. She thought of sneaking through that huge, dark, creaking house and cowered for a minute, then imagined waking him. She'd pull off his covers and he'd jump out of bed – then see it was her, and smile widely, in that way that showed off his teeth and made his eyes sparkle.

A giggle escaped her, and her fear was replaced by excitement. It was an excellent plan.

She slipped on her stockings to protect her feet from the cold floor, then tucked her doll under her arm and left the kitchen behind. Finding her way in the dark house was a little harder – and more frightening – without Levi's hand to hold, but she'd done it enough times by now that it wasn't long before she was climbing the long staircase, avoiding the two steps with the creaky banister by jumping soundlessly over them. The hallway with the paintings almost made her turn back. They were scary by candlelight; in the dark, she could just make out the pale shapes of their disembodied faces, and she could never quite look straight at all of them at once. It felt like the ones in the corners of her vision were moving.

Clutching her doll, Cara advanced one step at a time, the bright promise of Levi drawing her onward. Finally, blissfully, her hand was closing on the cold brass of the doorknob, and she twisted it open to slip into the room.

Levi wasn't asleep. The streetlight in the window lay across his pillow, and Cara saw that he was wide awake, staring up at the canopy of his bed, his eyes shining with tears. She knew then that something was horribly wrong, and the happy anticipation left her, replaced by a cold fear in the pit of her stomach.

"Levi?" Cara scampered across the floor, jumping onto the foot of the bed on her hands and knees. "Whatever is the matter?"

Levi sat up straight, blinking away the tears. His eyes widened. "What are you doing here?" he hissed, and his voice sounded strange and different. It was very hoarse.

Cara drew back. "I came like I do every night," she said. "I didn't know why you didn't come to fetch me."

"You can't be here, Cara," Levi hissed. His eyes flashed around the room, wild and scared.

"But I come every night." Cara heard her voice rising. "Why is tonight any different?"

Levi looked away. He moved his arms, and in the dark, Cara thought he was crossing them at first; then she saw that he was wrapping them around his body as if he was cold despite the fire that glowed softly in the hearth.

"You can't come here anymore, Cara," said Levi.

The words were like a blow so heavy that they didn't hurt at first, just left her feeling breathless and confused.

"What do you mean, I can't come?" she said. "Did Mama find out?"

Levi said nothing, but she saw his eyes filling with tears.

"Did she punish you, Levi?" Cara breathed.

"You just can't come up here anymore, all right?" said Levi. His voice was thick and harsh.

"Well... well, that's all right," said Cara. "We – we can play somewhere else, in the day. We can play in the stables, or on the lawn again."

"You don't understand," said Levi. "We can't play together anymore."

That was when the pain started to filter through, a steady throb that curled its hot tendrils around her heart. "Wh-why not?" Cara stammered. "Don't you like me anymore?"

"It's not that, Cara," said Levi. "We just can't play anymore." He grabbed his covers, pulling them up to his shoulders. "Now go away before Mama finds you."

"Levi, no." Cara pulled the covers back down again. "You can't do this. You have to tell me why you don't want to play with me anymore." Her voice sounded as raw as her heart felt.

"I can't," said Levi. "Just go away, Cara. Please."

"But you're my best friend," Cara whispered.

He sat up abruptly, and she saw tears rushing down his cheeks. "We're not friends at all," he said. "Not anymore."

She let him rip the covers out of her hands then, and as he bundled himself in them and turned with his back to her, she sat still for a few awful, long, cold moments until it sank in. It sank in like fangs into her flesh, a burning pain deep in her heart. She waited for him to apologize. She waited for him to realize what he'd done.

But Levi didn't move, and when Cara could, she fled. She pushed open the door, heedless of the sound of her feet on the floor and ran past the portraits that were nothing like as frightening as the reality that now faced her. She ran down the stairs two at a time and into the kitchen, curled herself up on her mat, and sobbed there until it felt her little heart would burst.

PART III

CHAPTER 16

Eight Years Later

Peeping sideways at the girl who stood beside her, her hands – like Cara's – buried deep in the dirty dish water, Cara figured that they had to be about the same age. Maisie had only been hired a week ago as a new scullery-maid, and the moment Betty had introduced her to Cara, she'd started to hope that perhaps life in the kitchen was going to be a little less lonely.

Still, as Cara kept dividing her attention between the plate she was scrubbing and the new scullery-maid, she felt a little daunted at the idea of talking to her for the first time. Maisie couldn't be any older than sixteen, yet her eyes held a hardness that Cara was more used to seeing in adults. She worked fast, her reddened hands swishing each plate through the water, giving it a brisk wipe with the dishcloth and placing it on the rising stack on the table.

Cara took a deep breath. Maisie looked up at her for a moment, and her little black eyes glittered at Cara dauntingly. She held out a hand, and for a strange moment, Cara thought she should take it. Then she remembered the plate in her hand. She handed it to Maisie, who plunged it into the rinse water without saying a word.

There were only two plates left. Cara didn't get to work with Maisie often, considering she spent most of her time helping Betty in the kitchen instead of the scullery, and if she wanted to talk to her, it was now or never.

She gathered her courage. "Lots of dishes tonight."

Maisie answered in a grunt, wiping down the plate.

Cara tried again. "Seems like there were a lot of guests at supper."

"Yes," said Maisie, bitterly. "And not one of them could finish up their good food." She shook her head. "Doesn't she know how many families are out there who'd give anything for a square meal?"

This had to be progress. Cara risked a smile. "It's dreadful, really," she said. "I can't believe they could be so wasteful."

"That's rich folk for you." Maisie held out a hand for the last plate. "Always cooking more than they can eat."

Cara was panicking. She'd at least started a conversation with Maisie, but she wanted desperately to take it a little further, to find some way of making friends with the only other child in the entire manor house.

"Yes, I suppose Glen and Edna wanted to show off," she said.

It was a mistake. The hardness returned to Maisie's eyes, and she stepped back, snatching the plate from Cara's hand.

"Glen and Edna is it?" she hissed.

Cara froze. She'd long since taught herself to stop calling Edna "Mama", but she realized, too late, that none of the other servants ever referred to the master and mistress of the house by their names – much less their first names.

"I..." Cara began.

"I didn't believe them when they told me that the mistress had taken you in as her own child," said Maisie harshly, "but now I do. What are you doing down here with the likes of us, then?"

"She didn't..." Cara tried again.

"You've never had to work a day in your life, have you?" Maisie spat. "You've never slept on the streets, cold and scared. You just get everything, and then you come down here and pretend that you're better than the rest of us."

The words stung. Cara worked in the kitchen just like everyone else. "That's not..." she began.

"Well, you're not going to win my trust," said Maisie. She plunked the last plate down on the stack, muscles rising on her wiry little arms. "I don't want nothing to do with someone like you."

She stormed out, leaving Cara alone in the scullery, tears prickling behind her eyes.

⚜

THE STABLES LOOKED different without Levi's pony in them. Cara figured she should be used to it by now; it had been years since the pony had been led away by his new owners, a trio of little girls with ribbons in their hair, giggling with excitement. Levi had wept that day, she knew, standing in the corner of the stable yard as tears coursed down his cheeks. She'd watched Glen put his arm around Levi's shoulders, telling him that he was a big boy now, too big for a pony, and that he'd soon forget all about the little creature once he'd gone off to boarding school – and later, university.

It had been years since Levi and Cara had spoken, but she'd still known that Glen was wrong. Levi would never forget that pony.

It hurt that he seemed to have forgotten *her* so easily.

She wandered across the cobbles, kicking at the bits of straw that blew this way and that in the fitful little wind, and left the stable yard and its sad memories behind, heading instead to the vegetable garden that now lay dormant beneath its covering of snow. Betty had told her not to mope over Maisie, or to let the girl's harsh words get under her skin. Cara knew Betty was right – she always was – but it felt like her wisdom was unattainable this time. Maisie's words had already gotten a lot deeper than just Cara's skin. She could feel loneliness all around her, wrapping her world in what felt like darkness.

The brisk clop of a four-in-hand trotting on the street ahead of them caught Cara's attention. Despite herself, she felt her heart speed up, pumping heat through her body. Could it be? They were early today, but she knew today was the day, and that was why she'd been hanging around outside instead of helping Betty in the kitchen – well, that and her desire to avoid Maisie.

Running over to the pine trees, Cara kept her body hidden behind one of the trunks, peering around it and through the thicket of needles to the facade of the manor house. The great palisade gates were swinging open, the ring of hooves sounding on the driveway, and Cara watched as Edna's gilded carriage made its way up to the great double doors. The four white horses came to a halt, the liveried footman pulled open the door, and Edna stepped out. Her figure was as slender as ever, unlike Betty's, which seemed to have softened and grown more rotund with the passage of the years; her hair, though silvery, was elegantly piled on top of her head. The change was in her face. Lines folded deep over her forehead, between her eyebrows, and around her mouth. There were very few around the corners of her eyes, because these days, Edna never smiled.

But it wasn't Edna that Cara was desperately looking at now. She held her breath as Glen followed her out of the carriage, and then, finally, he appeared. *Levi.* The only friend she'd ever had, and the one person who'd broken her heart more than any other.

He'd grown during his time at boarding school. She'd heard tell that the school was in the country somewhere; perhaps that was what had given him such broad shoulders and tanned his skin to a gleaming shade of golden bronze, but this last term at university hadn't been able to change his complexion. The windblown tufts of hair visible under his hat were laced with sunburned highlights of shining gold. His mouth quirked up at the corners, though, just as it had always done; and when he turned, the eyes that swept the lawn were still the same as ever. Brown and soft, deep as oceans, dark as midnight on Christmas Eve.

And they were looking right at her.

Cara's heart quickened. He was watching her, he was looking right at her, and for a moment he stood very still despite Edna, who was chattering in his ear. He took a step forward, one hand rising for an instant, and Cara felt her lips parting to call his name...

Then something changed in his face. A darkness fell over his eyes, and he stepped back, shaking his head, turning his back on her. His name died on her lips, and she watched him walk away from her like he'd done a thousand times before.

Dismay sucked the strength from her limbs. She sagged down into the snow, burying her face in her hands as the tears began to flow. She always looked forward to Levi's return for the holidays, and yet whenever he came back, it was always the same.

He broke her heart all over again.

CARA KNEW she was much too old to hold Betty's hand in the streets, but today, she'd made an exception. Clinging tightly to Betty, she stuck as close as she could to the cook, staring wide-eyed at the bustle of the marketplace. It seemed as though every cook in London had decided that today would be the perfect day to go out and do all their shopping for the Christmas feasts they were going to cook. Women were everywhere; some in cook's uniforms like Betty, others in their plain dresses, women who would be cooking for their own families. The square was packed full, queues of people waiting at every shop and stall.

"Maybe we should come back another day," said Betty, keeping a steady grip on Cara's hand. "This is madness."

Cara tightened the fingers of her free hand, feeling the edges of the small, round coin in her palm. Money was something that she almost never came by, and she was so excited to have a whole sixpence to herself that she couldn't imagine waiting a minute longer to spend it. She'd picked it up on the sidewalk a few days ago when she was taking the rubbish out to the bin men, and she'd been guarding it with her life ever since, knowing exactly what she was going to do with it.

"But it might be even worse another day, Betty," said Cara. "And we've walked all the way here already."

Betty sighed. "You have a point, child," she said. "My poor feet are already so sore and tired, a few hours of standing about in a queue won't make things much worse, I suppose."

She grumbled on as they moved slowly forward in the queue waiting to go into the butcher's. Cara could see the plump, neatly trussed geese displayed in the window. They made her think of the secret Christmas picnic she'd had on that miserable, yet wonderful Boxing Day morning right after Glen and Levi had found her starving in an alley. That had been turkey, not goose, but the memory always lurked right beneath the surface of her thoughts.

Her heart tugged at her, full and heavy as a grey storm cloud. There had been so much joy in that Christmas, yet it had all ended in tragedy, and she could feel herself growing listless as she stared at those perfectly plucked birds. They were just another symbol of the life she could never have. She wished she'd found Mama – her real mama – that Christmas. Then at least she'd have a family.

"Look at that," said Betty disapprovingly. "That young lady just picked the biggest turkey of the bunch. Doesn't she know that the medium-sized birds are more tender and flavourful? Someone ought to teach her how to be a proper cook."

Cara smiled despite Betty's grumpy tone. Betty was the closest thing she had to a family, and she squeezed the coin in her hand, reminded of what she was really doing here. "Can I be excused for a moment?" she asked.

Betty tightened her grip on Cara's hand. "Why, child?" she demanded. "I can't carry that goose and everything else myself, you know."

"You won't have to," said Cara meekly. "I'll come back as soon as I see you're going into the butcher's. I just saw a pretty dress in the window at the milliner's, and I wanted to look at it. Just for a minute."

Betty stared at her with those sharp eyes for a second, then relented. "I suppose you're not really a child anymore, are you?" she murmured. "Look at you. A young lady of sixteen, almost all grown up." She laid a loving hand on Cara's cheek, and for a moment the sourness left her face, replaced by a shining love. "Go on then. I'll see you in a minute."

"Thank you." Cara gave Betty a kiss on the cheek, making the grouchy old cook jump in surprise, and scampered off across the square.

The confectioner's shop was halfway down the opposite side of the square – close enough that Cara could squint through the crowd and still spot the front of the butcher's, and conveniently right next to the milliner's, but far enough that Betty wouldn't be able to hear her voice when she started speaking to the confectioner instead of the milliner. The queue in front of his shop was shorter. She stood half in it, half out of it, to look like she was looking at the dress, but instead her eyes were trained on the beautiful wares displayed in the confectioner's window. Piles of brightly colored candy canes – ever since her first Christmas at Edna's, Cara had never liked them. Toffee apples, round and bright and draped in dark, rich sugar. Mounds of white-dusted Turkish delight, just waiting to be bitten into to reveal the bright pink on the inside.

It was the chocolate, though, that had Cara's attention now. Betty loved chocolate. She was always breaking off tiny, tiny bits of the chocolate that was used to make Christmas coffee and licking her spoon as she baked chocolate cakes. One Christmas, Glen had given all the staff some drinking chocolate, and it had made Betty so happy that Cara had given her share to the cook.

But now she had something even better in mind – something *much* better than just a bit of drinking chocolate. She'd seen the advertisement in the newspaper. Between her lessons with Levi and a little effort from Betty, Cara could read passably well. They'd called it a "chocolate bar"; a whole stick of chocolate made just for eating. Betty would be over the moon.

It was new and expensive, but a sixpence would buy a small stick, and Cara was determined to give Betty a beautiful Christmas. She'd squirrel that chocolate away for the few weeks between now and Christmas Day, and she'd present it to Betty and see her eyes smile.

She was leaning forward, peering around the fat lady in front of her to look at the chocolate bars on display in the window in their bright wrappings, when it happened. A drunken tramp jostled one of the men in the crowd behind her. Cara heard him yell angrily and spun around just as he bumped into the woman in front of him, and in turn, she bumped into Cara. Off her balance, Cara staggered back, slipped on the sidewalk, and fell. With a yelp of surprise, she threw out a hand to catch herself – and the bright little sixpence fell from her fingers and rolled away across the street.

"No!" Cara cried, horrified as the little coin spun across the paving. Scrambling to her knees, she crawled after it desperately, heedless of the grimy ground. As she reached for it, it glanced off the shoe of a passer-by and spun away again, heading right for the grating over the gutter.

Cara let out a wordless yelp. She scrambled to her feet and ran after the sixpence, but it was already too late. It was right on the very edge of the grate...

A hand swooped down just as Cara lunged for the coin. Sweeping it safely away from the gutter, the grubby hand clutched the coin close to a ragged dress.

Cara straightened slowly, her heart pounding as she looked up. It was hard to tell just how old the woman was. Her face was lined and weathered, yet there were none of the sagging folds around her neck or jaw. Her figure looked young, but when Cara looked into her great, dark eyes, they looked older than London itself.

Cara held her breath. The woman's ragged clothing stirred in the breeze; she held a basket in one hand, a few sadly dried-out little holly wreaths lying at the bottom. She looked like she'd been trying to sell the wreaths on the street for a bit of money, and her pinched cheeks spoke of long starvation. Perhaps she was going to clasp that coin and run away. Cara could hardly blame her.

Instead, the woman was just staring at her for a moment that seemed to last a century. Then, slowly, she stepped forward and held out her withered hand, opening gnarled fingers to show the sixpence on her palm.

"Thank you," Cara breathed. She took the coin, feeling the warmth of the woman's skin when her fingertips brushed it. She knew that the queue at the confectioner's was getting longer, yet she couldn't seem to drag her eyes away from the flower seller. Something about her was tugging at the back of

Cara's mind, steady and insistent, refusing to let her walk away.

Perhaps it was pity. The woman looked so hopeless, so hungry. So lost. Cara glanced at the holly wreaths, slowly lowering her hand. "Do you have any flowers?" she asked.

The woman nodded. "Only dried ones," she said. She reached somewhere into the ragged folds of her clothing and pulled out a small, clear jar, containing a single dried rose. "Sixpence," she said.

"It's beautiful," said Cara. She held out the coin. "It'll make a lovely gift."

The woman smiled, and unexpectedly, her eyes shone brighter than Cara could have thought possible. She took the sixpence, letting out a wistful sigh that ended in a painful, hacking cough.

"Are you all right?" Cara asked.

"Beyond help," said the woman, "but thank you for brightening my day, little hummingbird."

CHAPTER 17

CARA WAS STILL THINKING about the strange woman days later as she buttoned her coat and grasped the handle of the rubbish bucket. It was a freezing day; the wind tossed angry blotches of snow against the windows as if the house had personally offended it somehow.

"Careful when you go out now," said Betty from where she was stirring the soup on the stove. "The ground will be frozen."

Cara smiled. "I've been taking out the rubbish since I was eight, Betty," she said. "I'll be careful."

"Oh, don't be snippy with me, you little hussy," grumbled Betty.

Cara laughed, thinking of the dried rose in its jar, which she'd wrapped in brown paper and hidden among the other modest little packages at the bottom of the Christmas tree that Betty had set up in the corner. That made her think of the woman again.

Hummingbird. Cara pushed open the back door, gasping at the gust of wind, and tightened her grip on the bucket's handle. Where had she heard that before? It felt like a memory, yet when she thought too hard, it seemed more like perhaps she'd been called that in a dream. Still, it haunted her.

Slipping across the cobbles, Cara hung on tightly to the bucket as she struggled across the back garden and through the stable yard to the alley at the back of the property where the rubbish men with their smelly cart would pick up the bin and tip it into the cart's filthy depths. She had to wrestle with the dustbin's lid for a minute; the wind seemed determined to wrench it out of her hands, and Cara just managed to keep it under control as she emptied the bucket. Slamming the lid back down over the stinking bin, she let out a breath of relief. Hopefully now she could spend the rest of the day safely in the warm kitchen.

That woman's eyes. They'd been so dark, so huge, and held such sorrow, yet something in them had lit up when they rested on Cara. She'd long since given up thinking about Mama. So why did that woman remind her so much of the mother she knew she'd never find again?

Clattering hooves shattered Cara's reverie, followed by a startled cry.

"Loose horse."

She looked up, raising a hand to shield her eyes from the blowing snow, and fear jolted through the length of her body. Rug flapping on its haunches, a horse was thundering across the stable yard toward her, its eyes wild and rolling white, lead rein swinging around its churning forelegs. It shied when it saw her, but its hooves slipped on the icy ground, and it went down heavily on one knee, a half-ton of thrashing limbs and panicked muscle sliding helplessly toward her. Cara scrambled to get out of the way, but it felt like running on soap. Her feet shot out from under her, and she saw the ground rushing up to meet her.

Something strong seized both of her shoulders. A heartbeat before the horse could crash into her, she found herself being plucked off her feet, lifted into the air and whisked around in a little half-circle that left her breathless. She was being held close to something warm and solid, and her fingers were clutching soft, thick fabric.

Heart hammering, she looked up into Levi's eyes.

It felt at that moment as if her racing heart simply stopped completely. Her breath certainly did; the steam hanging in the air between them came from between his parted lips. It had been years since she'd been so close to him, and she felt something now, something she'd never felt before even around

Levi. A tingling sensation, warm and bright as candlelight, threaded its way from the tips of her toes to the very top of her head. It filled her every vein with something that burned as pleasantly as the creamy, chocolatey Christmas coffee she made for the Halls each year. She wasn't sure what it was, but it didn't even seem to come from inside of her; it came from the depths of Levi's brown eyes and from the pressure of his hands on her arms and from the warmth of his body against her own.

She wished she could have frozen that moment in a snow globe and treasured it forever, but it ended like Christmas Eve, melting in the face of day. Levi stepped gracefully back, and his coat slipped through her fingers, yet his hands lingered on her arms.

She wanted to say his name, or anything really, but nothing would come out. Instead, it was his voice that spoke. It had broken a few years ago, and Cara had never heard it so clearly and so close in its new manly timbre before.

"Cara," he said. Her name sounded like molten honey on his lips.

"L-Levi." Reality crashed down around her. The last time he'd spoken to her, he'd told her that they could never play together again, and it was so many years ago, yet the pain of it was as fresh as a new burn. She tried to turn away, but his hands wouldn't let her, steady on her arms.

"Meet with me," he said, his voice warm and urgent.

"What?"

"Meet me tonight, here in the stable yard when it's past my parents' bedtime." His eyes never left hers.

She felt something new rise in her: suspicion. What did Levi want with her all of a sudden? "It's been years, Levi," she said.

"I know." Levi gave a sigh too long to be frustrated; it bordered on wistful. "But it feels like yesterday."

Cara's breath caught, because she knew exactly how she felt. Before she could think, she was answering him.

"All right," she whispered.

WHEN NIGHT CAME, it was the most perfect thing that Cara had ever seen; silver-bright, star-studded, snow-strewn, the stable yard so bathed in moonlight that she didn't need the flickering yellow glow from the candlestick in her hand. She clutched her coat closely around her throat as she ventured out of the kitchen. Banks of snow sparkled on either side of the footpath; salt crunched under her feet, staving off the ice that had caused the morning's incident. The horses were dozing, their heads over their half doors, sketched with lines of shining silver in the moonlight.

Cara could almost imagine the first Christmas being something like this. Bright and cold. Closing her eyes, she listened to the sound of the horses chewing, smelled the sweetness of their hay, rich with the floral memory of green summer. It was in a stable not unlike this one where Christmas itself was born and hope with it.

"I thought you mightn't come."

Cara startled. Turning, she saw Levi standing there like something between the shepherds and the angels. The moonlight touched his smooth skin with an almost ethereal glow, but it didn't touch his eyes. Those were the same as they'd always been; patient, kind, so gentle that they nearly brought Cara to tears. So gentle that they took her back to that night when she was only three years old, sobbing in her uncomfortable cot when he had just begun to supplant her.

The pain of the past years seemed to be washing away in the moonlight, but Cara still wrapped her arms around her chest as if to protect her heart from his onslaught.

"I thought you might not come," said Levi again.

"So did I," said Cara.

He thrust his hands into his pockets. Cara realized that he was wearing a suit; the jacket was unbuttoned, the collar carelessly open, his hair rumpled. He saw her staring and shrugged, giving her that smile that dimpled his cheeks so deeply. "Another of Mama's dinner parties," he said.

"So that didn't change," said Cara.

"Very little did, really." Levi took a step toward her.

She stepped back. "Except that eight years ago, you decided you didn't want anything to do with me anymore."

Levi looked away. "It wasn't my decision," he said.

"What do you mean?" asked Cara.

"I mean that I didn't tell you the truth back then," said Levi. "I should have, but I was too scared. I..." He reached a hand toward her, hesitated, let it fall back down by his side. "I couldn't let anything happen to you."

"Anything happen to me?" Cara shook her head. "I don't understand."

Levi looked over his shoulder, shivered a little, and shook his head. "Perhaps I'm mad even to think of telling you now... but no. You deserve the truth. I never had the courage to give it to you while I was a child, but a year at university has shown me that the world is bigger than I'd expected." He took a deep breath. "The truth is, Cara, I stopped talking to you because Mama forbade it."

Cara looked away, trying to cool the smarting pain in her heart. How could Edna's desires be so important to Levi that he'd throw away a friend so completely?

"It's not just that, either," Levi added hastily. "If I disobeyed her, she wouldn't just have punished me." He sucked in a breath. "She threatened to throw you out of the house."

Cara felt a jolt of cold run through her, strangely joined with a tingle of hope. She lifted her eyes to Levi's and saw tears glittering in them.

"I was afraid for you, Cara," said Levi. "I couldn't let that happen to you. But believe me, every time I've seen you in the past eight years, I've wanted nothing more than to run to you." He reached out again, keeping his hand open between them this time, like the hope of a promise to come. "That's why I was following you yesterday. I was hoping that you might pause by the street when you took out the rubbish so that we could talk somewhere that Mama couldn't see us."

Cara wasn't sure why there were tears running down her cheeks, but she knew that the emotion in her heart was more than just sorrow. "I've missed you so much," she whispered.

"I know." Levi bit his lip. "I've missed you too."

His hand was still open, held out to her, and Cara did at last what she'd been longing to do for years. She placed her hand inside his own and felt the warmth of his fingers curling around hers. He laughed slightly, a sound that was part sob. "I hope you can find a way to forgive me," he said.

"You were protecting me," said Cara, the wonderful truth filling her with joy. "You were caring for me all along."

She stepped to him, smelling his sweetness, which hadn't changed much over the years, and he took both of her hands in his own and squeezed them gently. She had to tip back her head now to look him in the eye, but oh, his eyes were the same. They were still so gentle, so deep, so breath-taking.

Levi leaned a little closer to her, and she was struck by how soft his lips looked when they parted as he spoke. "This time I will give you that Christmas I've been promising you," he whispered. "I'll be away at a friend's house for a few days starting tomorrow, but after that, I'm going to talk to my parents. I'm not a child anymore. I won't stand by and watch what's happening to you." He squeezed her hands. "I love you, Cara. I've always loved you, and I'm going to fulfill my promise at last. This Christmas you'll be part of the feast – for real, this time."

Cara's throat felt drawn tight with emotion so that she couldn't speak, but she hoped her eyes were telling Levi the truth that bounded in her heart; that she'd loved him ever since she'd set eyes on him all those years ago. It was so easy, so natural, to stand on tiptoe and lift her lips to his. And his kiss was light and brief and cool as the melting of a snowflake on her skin, but it lit up her whole world like the star of Bethlehem.

❧

AND FROM THE deep shadows between the house and stables, Edna Hall's eyes narrowed.

CHAPTER 18

CARA OFTEN HUMMED while she worked, but today, humming just wasn't good enough. Today she had to sing, and she let the words of the Christmas carol trickle from her lips as she kneaded a spongy ball of dough.

"O come, all ye faithful," she sang, "joyful and triumphant. O come ye, o come ye to Bethlehem."

"Oh, stop that racket, child," grumbled Betty from near the stove. "It's still a few weeks to Christmas."

Cara glanced over her shoulder. Betty's face was as grim as ever, but her eyes sparkled, and Cara laughed. "You like my singing," she said, flipping the dough over.

"You talk too much and work too little," said Betty, but her bitter words were laced with sweet good nature.

Cara kept singing as she kneaded the bread, unable to contain the flood of joy flowing through her heart like molten gold. Every cell in her body still felt like it was buzzing with the tide of emotion that had flooded through her at the touch of Levi's lips. He'd only stayed a moment after the kiss, gazing at her with those enchanting eyes, before disappearing back into the house, but the kiss lingered on. This time, Cara knew he'd make good on his promise. It was as he'd said: he wasn't a child anymore. He was eighteen, old enough to stand up to his parents.

Old enough to really change her life.

It felt as though he'd already changed it by finally telling her the truth. She parted the dough into three balls and started shaping one into a bread tin. Her heart felt so much lighter; it felt as though Christmas might be real for her this year, perhaps for the very first time. It was a pity that Levi was away for a few days now, but when he came back... She felt a smile lift her cheeks. When he came back, they'd finally be able to be together after all these years at a distance. Years that had failed to fade their affection for each other.

The creak of the kitchen door barely distracted Cara from her kneading, but the voice that rang through the room brought the entire kitchen to a standstill.

"You little *hussy*."

It was Edna, and her voice shrieked through the kitchen like fingernails on a washboard. Cara spun around just as the mistress of the house strode up to her, her finery brightly out of place in her utilitarian surroundings and raised an elegant hand.

"No," Betty cried, but there was no stopping Edna. The blow rang across Cara's cheekbone, a savage backhand that filled her mouth with the metallic taste of blood. She staggered back, too shocked to cry out, raising a hand to her face.

"Ma'am," Betty gasped, hurrying to Cara's side. Her warmth was reassuring; so was the steady grip of her hand on Cara's arm. "What's all this about?" she demanded, turning on Edna.

"I told you to stay away from my son," Edna hissed. Her eyes were wide, wild; a sharp contrast to the perfection of her clothes and hair. Tiny, foaming globs of saliva scattered from her mouth when she spoke. "But you insist on going near him. You insist on stealing his heart. His heart is *mine*. He is *my* child. *Mine*."

Cara barely recognized this woman as the sweet, soft-eyed lady that had first brought her to this house. She backed away, terrified, panic making her words scatter and stumble. "I... I didn't mean... I never..."

"You know exactly what you did." Edna shrieked. "I've tolerated you in this house for thirteen years, and this is how you repay me?"

"Cara didn't ask to be brought here, ma'am," said Betty, her words stony in their calm.

Edna ignored her as if she wasn't even there. "Well, I've had it with you and your promiscuity," she growled. Straightening herself, she raised an imperious finger, pointing it to the door. "Go."

Cara felt the world teeter under her feet. "G-go?" she stammered.

"You heard me," said Edna. "Get out of this house, and never come back. I never want to lay eyes on your wretched face again. Get away from my son and me – forever."

"Ma'am?" Betty gasped.

"Be silent," Edna yelled, rounding on Betty. "Do you want to be dismissed, too?"

Cara couldn't let that happen. She pulled her arm out of Betty's grip, feeling her body trembling. "All right. I'll go," she said. "Just don't dismiss Betty. Please, ma'am. None of this is her fault."

Edna's eyes glittered like frosted jewels as she glared at Cara. "Make yourself scarce," she spat, "or your precious cook will be out on her ear before you can think."

She turned and stalked away, her dress rustling up the steps into the house, and the door slammed behind her. Cara's knees seemed to lose their strength. She folded to the floor, a great sob ripping through her, and covered her face in her hands.

"Oh, Cara, Cara, my lamb." Betty wrapped her arms around her, drawing her back to her feet. "Hush now, hush. It's all right. I won't let her do this to you."

"You don't have a choice, Betty," Cara sobbed. "If you don't let me go, she'll dismiss you. And what will you do then?"

"I don't care," said Betty stoutly. "I'm not letting her get rid of you like this. It's not right. If you go, I'll go with you."

"No." Betty's words startled Cara clean out of her tears. Taking deep breaths, she gripped Betty's shoulders, straightening up. "Please, don't say that, Betty. Stay here." She thought of Levi and felt a jolt of hope. "Levi won't let this happen, either."

"He's not home," said Betty helplessly.

"Not now, but he'll be back. I... I can write a letter to him." Cara clenched her fists. "Would you give it to him?"

"Of course," said Betty. "And Edna won't know to stop you, because she doesn't know that you can read and write."

Cara nodded, trying to scrape together some semblance of courage.

"Where would you go?" said Betty.

"I don't know," Cara admitted. "But I'll keep writing. I'll find a way until Levi comes back." She took a shaky breath. "He came to find me before. He has to come and find me again."

"I hope you're right, lamb." Betty's eyes were dubious. "I truly hope so." Tears crept into her eyes. "But what will you do? Out on the streets, in the dead of winter..."

Cara felt the fear grip her, running through her body like rats, and she fought to keep it down. For Betty's sake, she tried to smile as well as she could. "I'll hope for a miracle," she said. "Christmas is the time of miracles, after all."

❧

CARA LEFT the letter with Betty, who only agreed to stay because she knew that giving Cara's letters to Levi was her only hope of returning to the Hall house and its warmth and food and safety. Then, with a little cloth bag on her back containing everything Betty could spare – some food, some money, and crucially, some paper and ink – she walked down the path beside the pine trees and out into the streets of London, alone, with no chance of ever turning back.

It was a lovely morning, with bright sun sparkling on fallen snow, but its beauty was lost on Cara. She only felt its cold, knowing how much colder it would be when the sun set, and fear gripped her.

She had to get a miracle for Christmas. It was her only chance not only at returning home, but at survival.

CHAPTER 19

GLEN WAS RELIEVED that the holidays had come at last. His business had been going full-tilt all year, more prosperous than ever, and while he was grateful for the success, exhaustion had been creeping up on him all year. Now he could finally get the rest that his doctor had been prescribing for months.

Stretched out on the chaise-lounge in the parlour, Glen took a sip from his glass of mulled wine, allowing its sweet warmth to spread all the way to his toes. He let out a sigh and tried to relax, reaching for the newspaper lying at his elbow as he listened to the homely crackle of the fire. But an undercurrent of stress was still running through his mind – not about his business, but about his home.

Glen abandoned the newspaper to rub his temples instead and took another, bigger, sip of the wine. Edna's behaviour had been strange for so long that Glen could hardly remember when it had all started. Years ago, he knew. His wife had always been a delicate creature, full of pernicious moods, and he had hoped so dearly – that fateful Christmas thirteen years ago – that the arrival of Cara and Levi would steady her.

It was a quiet tragedy in his life that the children seemed to have done the exact opposite. Especially Cara. He felt confusion clutch at his heart again as he remembered the day he came home from a trip to India to look into the nursery and find only one bright-eyed child waiting for him. Edna had told him that Levi and Cara were fighting, and that was why she'd moved the little girl into the kitchen. But that strange suspicion still filled him at times...

In truth, he'd tried more than once to restore the girl to their part of the house, but his wife had taken such a turn at each suggestion, that he'd finally given up. Something that haunted him regularly.

The smack of the parlour door swinging open made Glen jump. The wine glass rattled on the coffee table, then tipped over, spilling its rich contents over the newspaper that lay there. He uttered a quiet oath, swinging his feet down off the chaise-lounge and reaching for the paper, but the look on Edna's face froze him where he was.

She was standing in the doorway, her face scarlet, her eyes wild as long breaths made her chest heave, unladylike against the confines of her corset. Glen was on his feet before he could think.

"Edna!" he cried, startled. "What on earth is the matter? You look dreadful, my darling."

"That child," Edna barked. She swung the door shut with a slam that rattled the plaster, making Glen flinch. It was a sound he'd been hearing more and more often this holiday, shattering the peace of the home he'd been so proud to buy when he'd just married Edna.

"Levi?" said Glen, confused. "Isn't he at his friend's house until Thursday?"

"Not him." Edna strode back and forth across the carpet, her hands tugging distractedly at her curls, pulling them out of their elegant style into frizzing disarray. "*Cara*," she growled, spitting the name like it was poison.

"Cara?" Glen hadn't heard her even speak the girl's name in months. "What's happened?"

"She's stabbed me in the back," Edna growled. "She's stolen Levi's affection."

"Oh." Clarity dawned behind Glen's eyes. He'd seen the way their son had been gazing at Cara lately every time he was home, caught him often sitting by the window, watching as Cara swept the footpath or worked in the vegetable garden.

The look in Levi's eyes had been familiar. It was the same look that Glen had once given Edna.

Once. She'd been a different person then, and he struggled to find his affection for her now as she paced up and down their parlour. "Edna, darling, I know Cara isn't well-born," said Glen. "Not the type of girl we'd choose for Levi, and maybe we should talk to him about that, but..."

"I don't care about that." Edna's voice was as harsh as a creaking hinge. She spun to stare at Glen with eyes that looked ready to pop out of her skull. "You don't understand. She's *stolen* his love for me."

"What?" Glen shook his head. "What are you talking about?"

"That child has taken my son from me," Edna hissed. "She's made him love her even though I told him never to speak to her again."

"You did what?" said Glen, shocked. Cara and Levi had been practically siblings. How could Edna expect them not to be friends?

"Well, I've taught that traitorous little hussy a lesson," snapped Edna. "She won't show her face around here again."

Shock shot through Glen's heart. "What did you do?" he cried.

He hadn't meant to raise his voice, but it rang through the parlour, nonetheless. It seemed to take all the fire and fight out of Edna. She let out a sigh, her face turning grey, and sank down onto the armchair by the fire. Her eyes stared into the flames without seeing them.

Glen only just made out her next words. "Oh, you don't know what I've done," she whispered.

And no matter how much he questioned her about it, she refused to explain.

THE DAY WAS long and weary and cold and hungry. Cara tried to follow Betty's advice at first. "Whatever you do, you have to try to get a position at a manor house as a kitchen maid. You have some experience, and I've written you a letter of reference," she'd said, slipping it into the bag. "It's not much, a reference letter from a lowly cook, but it might help you. And at least you'll have somewhere warm to lay your head."

"Levi will come to find me," Cara had said.

"We don't know how long that will take," was Betty's response, and Cara hadn't liked the guarded edge in the cook's voice. It had started to wear down her hope, and as she trudged from one manor house to the next with her letter clutched hopefully in one hand, that hope wore ever thinner and thinner. One sour-faced housekeeper after the other opened the door to her, only to slam it again in her face. It was Advent, after all — the busiest time of a housekeeper's year. None of them had the time to listen to Cara's pleas.

And as the day wore on, the wind rose, and the sky grew ever greyer and heavier until Cara could nearly feel the leaden weight of it pressing down upon her. Still, her heart felt even heavier than that. She'd had so much hope when she'd stepped out of the house this morning, but in the face of this cold and the hunger that gnawed at her limbs, that hope had worn down to a pitiful little sliver. Levi felt a long way away; his kiss felt a hundred years ago.

She wrapped her arms around herself, gazing sightlessly around the street. She knew this part of London now, well enough to run errands by herself at times, yet it took her a second to recognize the marketplace where she and Betty so often came. There was the confectioner's, all bright with chocolate and candy canes; the butcher's shop had a few early turkeys in the window today. She still had the jar with the dried rose in her bag, in the hope that someday she could give it back to Betty. It was all so familiar, yet now that Cara knew that she wouldn't be walking home to a warm kitchen and Betty's smile, it all felt alien. Like she didn't belong here.

One thing was clear, at least, as she listened to the church bell chiming half past four. There would be no finding work today. She was stuck with sleeping on the streets tonight, and her heart gave a horrible little jump as she remembered the last time she'd slept in an alleyway, and the way the creeping darkness had filled her mind. If Levi hadn't found her when he did...

But he had found her. And he'd find her again. She had to believe that.

For now, she had to find somewhere to sleep. A shudder ran down her spine, and she shifted her bag on her shoulder, wondering if she should use a few of her coins to buy something for supper. But she'd eaten that morning. For how long would she have to do with one meal a day? The hunger nibbled at the inside of her stomach, but it would have to keep nibbling for now.

She was standing in front of the confectioner's now, gazing at the merry people buying gumdrops and gobstoppers inside, hardly able to believe that just a few days ago she was standing in a queue to get inside and buy some chocolate for Betty. That was when she'd dropped her sixpence and met the flower-seller with the dark eyes. An inexplicable wave of longing rushed through Cara, and she looked around, hoping to see the strange woman standing somewhere nearby.

But the marketplace was empty of her, and of any other friendly face, and Cara was alone – utterly, awfully alone.

She slunk into the alley behind the confectioner's, a narrow, dinghy gap with the shop on one side and what sounded like a family home or a tenement building on the other. People were talking and laughing and singing within, and Cara wished she could sing just to warm her heart a little, but no tune would come to her. There was nothing in this alley other than bits of old garbage and bins and the excrement of stray cats; it reeked with a stench that Cara didn't want to name, but at least it was out of the wind, and the overhang of the shop's roof would keep off some of the snow.

She wasn't sure that it would keep out the creeping cold that was already stiffening her joints and nipping at her fingers, but she had nowhere else to go. So she slipped into a gap between two garbage bins, ignoring their stench, closed her eyes, and prayed that the cold would wake her instead of killing her.

CHAPTER 20

IT WASN'T cold that woke her; it was voices, and a strangely sweet, yet dusty smell that was reminiscent of lavender. Cara's knees ached. Her hip was sore where it rested on the hard ground, and when she stirred, there was a painful crick in her neck from where she was resting her head against the wall. But she wasn't cold, she realized drowsily. She wasn't warm, exactly, but the happy crackle of a fire was nearby, and her limbs held none of that deathly numbness that she'd felt on the Christmas where she'd slept in the street.

"Look, Meg," said one of the voices. "She's awake."

Cara startled awake at the proximity of the voice. The first thing she saw was a pair of small, bright eyes, beady as a bird's, staring directly into her own from either side of a hooked and reddened nose. They were so intense that Cara let out a little yelp and scrambled to her feet. A thickly knitted shawl fell away from her shoulders as she moved, landing in a rumpled heap at her feet.

"And quite lively, by the looks of it," the owner of the hooked nose stated. She was a tiny little old woman, so bent and frail that she looked like she'd been made from dry sticks and bits of wire. Now that Cara was half awake, she realized that she was head and shoulders taller than the old lady.

"See?" grumbled the second voice. "She's all right. We needn't have gone to the trouble."

Cara looked up. There was another figure huddled by the little fire that had been made in the alley. This woman was a little younger than the other, with a roomy, curvy figure that might have been portly once, before poverty had stolen the rich lines of her body and left her looking bony and gawky. She prodded at the fire with a stick, then looked up at Cara, her greying curls sagging lifelessly from under a yellowed bonnet.

"Don't you listen to her, pet," said the older woman. She patted Cara's hand with a curved claw. "She's got a kind heart really, our Margaret. Besides, it was no trouble to make our fire near you. We had to make it somewhere, didn't we?"

"Who... who are you?" said Cara, confused. She felt a little like these two old ladies weren't real at all.

"Oh, I'm Livia," said the older one. She beamed up at Cara with a mouth full of loose, yellow teeth. "And this is Margaret."

"Hello?" said Cara uncertainly. She glanced around the alley, then back down at the blanket lying at her feet, then into Livia's wobbling smile. "Did... did you cover me with the blanket?" she said.

"Nearly froze to death because of it," grouched Margaret.

"Of course, we did, pet," said Livia. "Couldn't let a scrap like you freeze to death, could we?"

Cara felt her shoulders relaxing a little. "Thank you," she said. She glanced around for her bag, snatching it up almost instinctively, relieved to hear the soft jingle of coins. Her stomach felt as empty as her heart.

Margaret looked up at the sound of the coins, her eyes widening. Livia perked up similarly. "Oh, you've got some money?" she said. "Why don't you buy a posy?"

"A what?" said Cara, thoroughly confused.

"A posy," said Livia. "Show her, Meg, dear."

Margaret reached into a closed wicker basket by her side and morosely pulled out a little knot of flowers, held together by a doily made from bits of string. It was a sad-looking little thing, reminding Cara of the wreaths that the flower-seller from the other day had been selling, but she forced a look of wonder onto her face.

"Oh, it's lovely." she said. "I'm afraid I... I can't, though." The weight of her situation crashed down onto her shoulders, and she blinked back tears. "I have to start looking for work. I have nowhere to go."

"Oh, neither do we," said Livia comfortably, "but we sell our posies and we get by, don't we, Meg?"

"Depends what you mean by 'getting by'," said Meg. "We eat sometimes and we ain't froze to death yet."

Looking at their deeply creased, weathered faces, Cara wondered how long they'd been living like this. Two poor little old ladies, wandering the streets in the pitiless winter, hopelessly trying to sell their tiny knots of flowers. It made her heart ache and throb with terror at the same time. Was this her future?

She had to believe in Levi.

"It's better than some people have, Meg," Livia was saying. "Don't be so dour. It's Christmastime – try to be a little jolly, why don't you?"

"Christmastime?" Margaret spat noisily onto the fire, making it splutter. "Same as any other time of year, except cold. Nobody's buying posies from old street sellers. Everyone's saved up their money for finer gifts. Besides, there ain't no flowers no more. Can hardly get any posies *to* sell. I'm surprised every time we survive it."

"Oh, Meg." Livia sighed, shaking her head. But as she looked up at Cara, something of her cheerfulness left her eyes, and a sorrow crept in that hadn't been there before. "It's not right, though," she said sadly. "A pretty little young thing like you, on the streets at this time of year. There's dangers out there for you, pet. Stay away from men – even rich men, and especially drunken ones."

The implication in her tone slithered coldly down Cara's back, like dirty snow. "I'm scared," she admitted. It was a danger she hadn't thought of, and she'd thought of many.

"Then stay with us," said Livia.

"What?" said Margaret sharply.

"Don't be like that, Meg," said Livia. "You know that a pretty face would only help us, and you're right – we've hardly sold a thing in the past two days. Maybe people will buy them from this lovely girl instead of us wrinkled old bags."

"Who're you calling an old bag?" said Meg, but her eyes were calculating as they rested on Cara, and she finally nodded. "Maybe," she said.

"Oh, would you let me come with you?" Cara said. "I – I'll make myself useful. I'll carry things for you and sell as many posies as I can. I just..." She swallowed. "I don't want to spend another night on the streets alone." She was well aware that she may not have survived last night at all if it wasn't for these two old ladies and their kindness.

"That's settled, then," said Livia. She stood up, reaching for the basket. "Put out the fire, Meg. Let's sell some posies. What's your name, by the way, pet?"

"Cara. Cara Cooper."

"Cara, Cara." Livia hesitated, sucking on the inside of her cheek in thought. "Now where have I heard that lovely name before?" There was a long pause as the world waited for Livia to think, but eventually, she shrugged and smiled. "It doesn't matter. Let's go."

LEVI HAD KNOWN that something was wrong from the moment he stepped out of his friend's carriage, waved a last goodbye to the rowdy gang of young men crowded into the vehicle, and mounted the steps to the great front doors of his home. Mama hadn't been waiting for him at the door.

It was strange, but not strange enough to frighten him, Levi told himself. It was dinnertime; maybe Papa had convinced Mama to sit down at the table and eat for once, instead of picking at her food, slurping at her wine, and then retiring early, saying she had a headache. Maybe Mama had even forgotten he was coming home today. It would be a relief more than anything if that was true; he'd long since grown tired of the obsessive way she tracked every move he ever made.

"I'm home," he called out, allowing the butler to slide off his coat.

"In here," Papa's voice called. There was a tightness in it that Levi didn't like at all. He moved quickly, striding into the dining hall, and saw that the staff had already selected a Christmas tree. It stood in one corner, bare and beautiful in its way despite its lack of decorations, its dark boughs a shadow against the patterned wallpaper.

Papa was sitting at the head of the table, a half-finished bowl of mushroom soup in front of him, and there were dark circles under his eyes. That was unusual for this time of year – normally this was one of the few times that Papa was home and resting. But it was the look on Mama's face that really frightened him. Her eyes only flashed up to meet his, then slid away again, darting to and fro in her pale face. Her soup sat untouched on the table.

Levi forced himself to be cheerful. He couldn't let his parents get in the way of the joy that this Christmas was going to bring him. Excitement ran through him; this was the Christmas that he was finally going to fulfill his promise to Cara, no matter what it took. He couldn't wait to hurry down to the kitchen after supper and see her.

"Good evening," he said brightly. There was a place set for him opposite Mama; he slid into the chair, forcing a smile. "I'm sorry I'm late to supper."

"It's all right, son," said Papa, smiling at him, but his eyes were tired and wary.

"Good evening," said Mama, her voice thin and strange. She grabbed her spoon, gulped a mouthful of soup, then set it down again.

She was acting even stranger than normal, and that was saying something, given how strangely she'd been acting ever since Levi could remember. He turned to Papa instead, feeling that churn in his stomach again as he saw the look in his father's eyes. Not knowing what to say, he tasted his soup as well, feeling the silence press down on his shoulders. What was going on?

The air felt tight and hot, like it might explode at any minute, and Levi could hardly bear it as he raced through the meal as quickly as he could. The pause between each course felt like it lasted a century. He bolted the last few bites of the chocolate pudding they had for dessert, then set down his fork neatly and looked up at Papa.

"May I be excused?" he asked.

Mama looked up at him as sharply as if he'd cursed. But Papa shot her a warning look, then nodded. "Of course, son. Wouldn't you like to have some coffee with us in the parlour?"

Levi wanted nothing other than to see Cara, to feel the curves of her body pressed against his own again, to taste her sweet lips. "I'll join you a little later," he said, trying to make his tone as light as possible.

"Why not now?" snapped Mama, testily.

"That's enough, Edna," said Papa.

Levi stared at him. He'd never heard Papa use that tone with Mama before; there was no rage in it, but there was a finality that made her eyes widen. But he had bigger things to worry about than his parents right now. He pushed back his chair and left the dining hall, using the door that led to the main hall and the stairs so that his parents wouldn't be suspicious. Instead of climbing the staircase, though, he went out of the front door, closing it quietly behind him.

Once he was outside in the crisp air, he couldn't hold back his excitement anymore. Laughing with joy and anticipation, Levi jogged across the crunching snow of the lawn, ducked between the pine trees, and started up the path through the vegetable garden and into the kitchen.

"Cara, my darling," he sang out as he reached for the back door. "I'm back."

He pushed it open and stepped into the warmth of the kitchen. Betty was standing at the kitchen table, and when he came in, a look of relief flooded through her pleasantly ugly features. "Levi," she gasped. "You've come back."

"Hello, Betty." Levi beamed at her. "Busy with the plum pudding for next year, I see."

"Never you mind the plum pudding," said Betty. "There's more important things to worry about now." She pushed the mixing bowl aside and strode up to him, groping around in the front pocket of her apron. "Read this at once," she said, pulling out a creased, folded envelope.

Levi felt his laughter die in his chest as he saw the look in Betty's eyes. He took the envelope from her, his heart suddenly pounding. "What's going on, Betty?"

"Just you read it." Betty's voice sounded choked with tears. "Read it and put things right, Levi." She reached out, grasping him by the lapels of his suit, an inexcusable act that frightened him even more as she spoke intensely into his face. "I don't know if anyone can fix this," she said, "but you had better try, my boy. You had better be the Christmas miracle that Cara needs."

The excitement in Levi's heart was abruptly snuffed out. He ripped open the envelope and scanned the letter as quickly as he could, picking his way through the loopy, childlike script.

DEAR LEVI,

Edna has sent me away. She saw us together. I'm scared.

I know you promised we would have Christmas together this year. I trust you.

I don't know where I'm going, but please find me.

Love,

Cara

LEVI FELT as though his blood was on fire. He lowered the letter in a trembling hand and stared wordlessly at Betty.

"Be her miracle," the cook repeated.

Levi spun on his heel and ran back toward the house, feeling his body shake with rage. When he reached the dining hall and flung the doors open, it was empty, and that only made him angrier. Storming upstairs to the parlour, he could see Mama and Papa through the open door. Papa was leaning back in his armchair, reading the newspaper; Mama sat on the chaise-lounge, biting her nails, and he felt a hot bolt of rage pulse through him at the sight of her.

"What have you done?" Levi heard himself yell as he pushed the door open.

They both jumped. Papa lowered his newspaper, anger flashing in his eyes. "Levi," he said, "don't raise your voice at your mother like that."

"I'm sorry," Levi ground out through gritted teeth, even though he wasn't. "I just want to know what's happened to Cara."

Mama flinched at the name as though he'd struck her. "And why do you want to know that?" she said, glaring up at Levi. "Don't ask such silly questions about a simple maidservant, Levi. How dare you speak to me like that?"

Levi wanted to yell at her, but out of respect for his father, he didn't. He was still trying to formulate a polite answer when Papa spoke up.

"She's not a simple maidservant, Edna," he said. His voice was calm, but Levi could hear anger trembling just beneath its surface. "You know that. She was supposed to be our daughter." An aching confusion filled Papa's eyes as he set aside his newspaper. "Why did you put her aside like that?"

Levi stared at him. He'd never heard Papa question Mama like this before, and Mama looked just as surprised. Her lips parted. "I... I..." she stammered.

"Why did you chase Cara away, Mama?" Levi brandished the letter.

"What's that?" said Mama sharply.

"A letter she gave me," said Levi.

"I told you never to talk to that girl." Mama barked.

"And why did you do that?" asked Papa, so quickly that Mama sat back, blinking at him. "She was meant to be his sister, Edna. Now you're treating her like an enemy."

"I don't understand that either," said Levi. "Why did she call you Mama, when we were little? She still called you that even after she moved – even after *you* made her move out to the kitchen. Why did she live in the nursery for such a little while?"

"You two were fighting," said Mama.

"We never fought," said Levi. "I loved having her there. And now..." He stopped, aware that he was breathless, his chest heaving. "And now I love her, Mama," he said. "I love her in a way that I've never loved anyone, no matter how hard I tried to forget her while I was at school."

There was a moment of ringing silence. Papa's eyes were dubious, but not surprised, and Levi felt a moment's regret about his outburst. He knew that Papa wanted him to marry well. The look in Mama's face, though, quickly consumed his thoughts. She looked horrified – no, more than that. She looked appalled, her face utterly grey, her eyes wide with anger and disgust.

"How *dare* you love her," Mama growled, rising to her feet. "How *dare* you love her and hate me."

"I don't hate you," said Levi, hurt and confused by her words. "I'd never hate you, Mama. I just don't understand why you treat Cara like this."

"I'm sorry, my love, but I have to agree with Levi," said Papa, his voice growing gentler. "Why did you reject little Cara when you adopted her from the workhouse, just like I did with Levi?"

"Why can't you just let us be together?" Levi cried.

Their onslaught seemed to suddenly become too much for Mama. She clapped her hands over her ears, letting out a cry. "I hate her because I stole her!" she yelled.

The words left Levi feeling stunned, as if he'd just been struck. Judging by the look on Papa's pale face, he felt the same. The silence enveloped the parlour, and horror filled Levi so tightly that it choked the words out of him. He couldn't seem to move.

Papa's voice was shaking when he spoke. "Excuse me?" he said. "You... you *stole* Cara?"

Mama collapsed into an armchair, covering her face with her hands, and huge sobs came boiling out of her that shook her entire body. Part of Levi wanted to run to her and wrap his arms around her, but he was rooted to the spot.

"What do you mean by this?" Papa's voice was agonized. "Edna, what did you do?"

"I took her," Mama cried, lowering her hands to reveal wet, wild eyes. "She was some kitchen maid's child, and I wanted her. I *wanted* her, Glen, and what life would a kitchen maid have given that little girl? So I took her."

Levi felt as though the world was spinning out from under his feet. Suddenly, Cara's ramblings when she was a little girl were making sense. He'd always thought that she didn't remember her time in the workhouse, or if she did, that the hatefulness of that time had made her forget it; he wished often that he could forget his own few years in that awful place. "You stole Cara *from her mother?*" he croaked.

"It was for her own good." Mama yelled.

Papa said nothing. He rose from his seat, his face ashen, and strode out of the room.

"Glen!" Mama shouted.

"How could you, Mama?" Levi gasped, his voice trembling. "How could you do something so awful? Steal a child and then reject her?"

"Levi, my darling..." Mama held out a hand to him.

Levi dodged it, shaking his head. "Don't touch me," he muttered, turned around, and followed his father outside.

CHAPTER 21

CARA WOULDN'T HAVE KNOWN that it was Christmas Eve at all if it wasn't for the cries of "Merry Christmas" ringing cheerfully back and forth across the bleak, frigid street. The decorations on the shop doors, the candles in the windows, the carollers in the streets – they'd all been there for days. So had the angry looks, the scowls and kicks aimed in her direction, the men who'd give her greasy looks while she trembled on a street corner, a few dry and tattered posies held up in one hand.

Days, weeks... Cara didn't know how long she'd been staying with Livia and Margaret, but she knew that it was long enough that hunger had stolen the padding from her bones, leaving them jutting against her skin like Margaret's. They never slept in the same alley twice; moving constantly was the only way they could keep safe, Livia said. Cara supposed she was right, but she also knew the constant movement was making it harder and harder for Levi to find her. She'd written a few letters addressed to the Halls' house, but there had never been enough money to post them. Eventually, she'd sold her paper and ink to buy food.

Now, there was no money left, and no food either. Her only hope was to sell a few posies before night fell and everyone went to their homes and their Christmas dinners and their children and their warm fires. Holding up a couple of posies, she ignored the way her teeth were chattering in the icy wind and raised her voice as well as she could.

"Lovely posies!" she cried out. "Pretty posies. Last-minute gifts. Only tuppence for three." It had been tuppence for one, a few days ago, but Cara was growing desperate. She spotted a ragged-looking man scuttling across the street and strode desperately toward him, holding up the posies. "A lovely gift for your lady wife, sir," she cried.

He spat. The nasty, greyish glob sailed through the air and landed on her dress with a disgusting *splat*. "Ain't got no wife," he growled.

"A daughter?" Cara tried valiantly.

He slammed a grubby hand, its nails long and yellow, into her shoulder.

"Get away," he barked, spraying spittle in her face. Cara stumbled and fell backwards, grasping the posies desperately, landing heavily on her rear. The posies crunched in her hands, and she gave a yelp of dismay as the man scuttled off. They'd been bent and crushed beyond repair in her fall, and she felt tears sting her eyes.

"Oh, pet, pet." Livia's voice was soothing when her little claws closed around Cara's hands and drew her to her feet. "Don't you mind him. He's got no Christmas spirit in him at all, nasty old man."

Cara blinked back her tears as Livia dusted some snow off her skirt. "I'm so sorry about the posies," she said. "I want to help you and Meg, but I've been failing you both."

"Not a bit of it, darling," said Livia. "Come now. That's enough for one day. Meg's built a fire in that house over there – it's been abandoned for years. Let's go sit down."

"But we have nothing to eat," said Cara. "And it's Christmas Eve. We haven't eaten all day. We have nothing."

"We'll find something tomorrow," said Livia, wobbling her wrinkles up into a smile. "And we don't have nothing, do we, darling child? We have each other."

It was something, Cara supposed, but as Livia led her toward the burned-out shell of some old building – its inside eerily lit up by the glow of the tiny fire Margaret had composed from the few bits of damp coal they'd scavenged from behind a smithy – her loneliness was still even more cold and keen than the hunger that pierced her from head to toe. She loved the two old ladies, but they weren't Levi.

Levi. Pain hummed through her. He'd promised her a beautiful Christmas, and here she was, spending Christmas Eve homeless and hungry. He'd broken his promise before, she knew. Yet deep in her soul, she trusted him, and she didn't know why.

It was for that reason that Cara managed to smile at all as Livia led her over to the fire and she sat down opposite Margaret, and they drank melted snow from a cracked piece of clay pot while Livia chattered incessantly and even sang a couple of tuneless Christmas carols. Margaret was silent and dour; Cara sat in a sunken heap of despair, trying to smile at Livia's bad jokes and wayward stories. Livia loved to tell stories, her hands dancing in front of her, her eyes alive, but she seldom ever remembered what she was doing long enough to actually reach the end of any story. Instead, she plaited little fragments of stories together like daisy chains, her voice pattering optimistically onward. Cara wondered how many long, hungry nights she'd whittled away like this for herself and Margaret.

Her eyelids were growing heavy, exhaustion slowly winning out over hunger, when she heard her name. Blinking, she sat up. "I'm sorry, Livia," she said. "What were you saying?"

"I was saying that I finally remember where I've heard your pretty, pretty name before, pet," said Livia. "*Cara* – it's such a lovely name. I never knew anyone else called Cara, but I've heard that name before a hundred times. Why, I'm surprised I didn't remember it until now."

Cara wasn't overly surprised; Livia could seldom remember what day of the week it was or their price for posies. "Oh?" she said, trying to act interested for Livia's sake. "Where did you hear it before, then?"

"It was Vickey's daughter's name," said Livia happily.

Something hot and electrifying shot through Cara's veins. She sat bolt upright. "Vickey?" she gasped. "You knew someone called Vickey?"

"Oh, yes, pet," said Livia. "A lovely, lovely girl she was, absolutely lovely. Sold posies with us for years and years. I miss her dreadfully, so I do. She was a regular angel. Sad, poor thing, but she'd been through so much. She was always talking about her little daughter, Cara, who she lost."

"Lost?" Cara felt herself trembling.

"Yes – the child just plain disappeared. She thought her mistress' sister had something to do with it, but she could never prove anything, or find the poor mite. She spent her whole life searching for little Cara. Even though she must be all grown-up by now."

Cara swallowed hard. Could it be? Had she found her after all these years?

"My mother was called Vickey," she breathed.

"That's nice," said Livia. "Vickey's such a pretty name, too. Why, I loved our poor Vickey. There was this time that…"

Margaret cut her off abruptly, her sharp eyes staring into Cara. "Your mother," she said. "Did she have dark eyes? Dark hair?"

"Very dark," said Cara. "Like mine." She touched her own cheek. "She… she was so kind. She lost me when I was just three years old. I was taken from her."

"How awful," cried Livia.

"Liv." Margaret turned to her. "Don't you see? This is *that* Cara – *Vickey's* Cara. We've found her. We've found her at last."

Livia fell suddenly silent. Staring at Cara with round, sparkling eyes, she let out a gasp, clasping both hands over her mouth. "So it is," she said. "I wondered why I thought she was such a nice-looking girl when we first found her. Why, Meg, she has Vickey's eyes."

Cara felt them fill with tears. "Oh, Livia, Livia," she cried, scrambling to her feet, seizing the old woman's little claw-like hands in her own. "Please, tell me where she is. Tell me where I can find Vickey – where I can find *Mama*."

Silence fell but for the crackle of the fire, and Livia and Margaret exchanged a glance. And the heaviness of that silence told Cara the awful answer to her question.

CHAPTER 22

THE SNOW WAS FALLING TOO QUICKLY to be pretty. There were no sparkles on the snowflakes tonight; in fact, they hardly felt like individual flakes at all. Instead, they came down in a long grey sheet, cold and muffling, making it feel difficult to breathe as they brushed across Cara's face. She had to crouch down to see the scar of the fresh dirt in the church-yard, already hard with frost.

Tears dripped down her cheeks, feeling so cold that they might freeze to her skin any moment. Cara sagged to the cold ground, her knees curled up underneath her. Her body was too tired and hungry to sob, so she just listened to the soft patter of her falling tears and thought about how truly alone she had become in this world.

Inside the church, she could hear Christmas carols being sung. Rich folk were standing up in the pews, looking up at the Nativity scene by the altar, smiling as they worshiped under the rich gold of candlelight. Christmas Day had come for them, but not for Cara. Not if Christmas was a time of miracles.

The miracles had all run out for her. Had they ever even started?

She pressed her hands into the fresh dirt, barely able to feel it with her numb fingers, and allowed her tears to flow unchecked.

"I'm so sorry, love." Livia hobbled a little closer, resting a hand on Cara's shoulder.

"I miss her." Cara's words sounded like broken pieces of her heart tumbling out of her. "I've missed her all my life, and now I'll never stop."

"It was the consumption that took her," said Margaret. "She fought hard. We did our best."

"It was just a few days before you found us," said Livia. "I know she would have held on for you, if she'd known."

Cara bowed her head, feeling like her despair was too heavy for her bones to carry. She pressed her forehead to the dirt, wishing she could be pressing herself into her mother's arms instead of into her grave. Livia and Margaret had told her everything as they walked up to this churchyard, about how they'd found Mama half-starved and freezing many years ago, how she'd told them that her mistress had dismissed her for searching for her stolen daughter. She knew now that that mistress had to be awful Aunt Giselle that Levi hated so much.

Levi. Cara squeezed her eyes shut, sending a fresh burst of tears down her cheeks. It was Christmas now, and once again, she wouldn't be feasting in the decorated dining hall. She'd be out on these streets, scared, starving, and now, grieving. Grieving the mother who'd spent her life searching for her.

"Oh, Mama, Mama, Mama," Cara whispered, her voice thick with tears. "Oh, Mama, I miss you."

"I'm so sorry," said Margaret, her voice tender for the first time. "We tried to help her."

"But in the end, all we could do was put her in a pauper's grave." Livia's voice cracked. "Oh, Meg, if only she could have seen poor Cara once before she died."

Cara had been too late. And as cold and weakness seeped into her bones, she knew that Levi was too late, too.

There would be no miracles this Christmas. In fact, Cara wasn't sure that miracles even existed. She couldn't trust in them. She couldn't trust in Christmas.

And even more than that, she could never again trust in Levi Hall.

IN THE BRUTAL economy of hunger, there was little room for despair. Cara would gladly have lain on that cold earth until the snow covered her, until the cold claimed her at last and slipped her away from the world that had become so cruel, but she knew that Livia and Margaret were quietly starving. They were all she had left. They were all that had kept her mother alive for years, and she had to do something to help them.

So it was, as Christmas services ended and people returned to their warm homes and jolly gifts, that Cara was following a portly man down a middle-class street as he and his family bustled down the sidewalk. She assumed they were coming from church; everyone was dressed to the nines, the man in his shiny bowler hat, the woman neat in her dress and boots, and the three children all scrubbed and stuffed into uncomfortable clothes. It wasn't the clothes that Cara cared about right now, though. It was the parcel under the woman's arm. She guessed it must be a gift from someone at church, or maybe something she was taking to a friend's house, but she didn't really care which. All she knew was that there were grease stains on the brown paper, and it smelled wonderful. Fresh bread, perhaps, or fish, or anything. She would have gladly eaten the paper itself, she was so hungry.

She tried not to think about what she had to do. It was this, or starve, and she couldn't think of the implications.

All she needed now was a distraction – a moment that the father wasn't looking adoringly over at his wife with her parcel. It presented itself perfectly when the littlest of the children, a girl with plump blonde pigtails, tripped over a crack in the pavement. She landed heavily on one knee with a yelp, and immediately began to howl, her chubby cheeks brick red. The father turned, extending his hands to her, and the mother stopped in her tracks.

It was the chance that Cara needed. She rushed forward, her hands held out, and before the mother could whirl around, her fingers were closing on the brown paper. The woman let out a shriek, clutching at the parcel, but Cara's hunger had given her strength. She ripped at it, yanking it out of the woman's hands, a long tear in the paper letting out a burst of savoury scent.

"Stop!" the woman cried. "No. That's for Christmas."

Cara didn't care about Christmas. She didn't care about anything but her hunger, and she clutched the warm parcel close to her, bolting down the street as fast as her legs could carry her.

"Stop thief!" screamed the father's voice behind her. "STOP!"

Cara kept running, her breath ragged, her limbs aching, but she had to get away. More voices had joined the family's cries, and there were feet pounding after her, and she could do nothing but run and pray that no one would catch her. But the strength of terror and desperation couldn't last, not with only an empty stomach to drive them on. She could feel her legs growing weaker and weaker as she fled, her feet wobbling on the slippery street. Her vision was growing dim, and she could barely hear the shouts of her pursuers through the ringing in her ears.

She wasn't sure how she fell. Perhaps someone tripped her, or she tripped on the sidewalk, or maybe her legs just gave in. She just knew that she was falling, her cheekbone smashing into the hard paving with a force that made a terrible crunching sound, and that angry hands were plucking at her clothes. A foot slammed into her ribs with a bloom of pain, and Cara rolled onto her side, still clinging to the parcel and its wonderful vinegar smell of fish and chips. They were being crushed now, mashed and mixed into the grubby street, as voices yelled, and she was kicked and pulled around.

She half wished that they would kill her. She wished that it would just stop, that there would be no more hunger or fear or Christmas, that she could just sleep and be left alone in the darkness...

"Stop. Stop that at once!"

The voice was familiar, in a way, but Cara couldn't place it. It was a dim realization through the fog of pain and semi-consciousness, and she didn't really care. She just wanted to rest. It was a relief when the pulling and kicking stopped, but she couldn't even feel dismay when she realized that the parcel had gone from her arms. It didn't matter anymore. Nothing really did.

Nothing except the voice that spoke above her, a blinding ray of brilliant light piercing her despair.

"Cara, it's me. I've come to find you."

She opened her eyes, and somehow, he was there. Leaning over her, his eyes shining with love and tears, his big hands closing on her shoulders.

"Levi?" she breathed.

"I'm so sorry. Oh, Cara, I'm so sorry. I was nearly too late."

She couldn't speak. She was being pulled into a pair of strong arms, against a warm and solid chest, her head tucked into the crook between his neck and jaw, and Cara couldn't believe that this was real. She must be dreaming. She might be dead. But she could feel his heartbeat against her as he held her, cradling her, and the rumble in his chest as he apologized over and over, stroking her hair.

"Levi?" she said again.

"I'm here." Levi cupped a hand over her head, pulling her close to him. "I'm right here, and I'm never leaving you again, never."

"You found me," Cara managed.

"Of course, I found you. I promised you I'd bring you home for Christmas, didn't I?"

She pulled back a little so that she could look into his eyes, into his deep, gentle eyes and feel a deep shame as she realized that she'd stopped trusting him. Tears blurred her vision, and she found the strength to push him away, to scramble to her feet. She was horribly aware of her filthy, ripped dress, of her bruises, of her shame lying in the street with a crushed parcel of fish and chips.

"I'm nothing," she cried. "I'm nothing. Please, leave me." She turned to run, and nearly ran straight into Glen, who gripped her shoulders with gentle hands and studied her over his sandy little moustache.

"No," said Glen. "We're not leaving you again, Cara. Our family has left you quite enough. If anyone should feel shame, it's Edna... and me." Guilt filled his eyes. "I should never have let this happen to you."

Levi grasped her hand softly. "Cara, please," he said. "Please. I've been searching for you for weeks and weeks. Believe me when I say that I love you."

She turned to him then, and looked into his eyes, searching for hope in them, for family, for everything she'd ever longed for. And she didn't find it then, but when he pulled her closer and pressed his lips to her own for a glorious instant, that was when the golden bells of Christmas rang at last in her heart.

"Let me give you the Christmas you've always been waiting for," Levi whispered.

"LET GO OF HER."

The shriek was high-pitched, accompanied by the rapid staccato of wobbly feet on the paving, and Cara pulled back in time to see Livia descending upon them. The old woman's wild hair was blowing in the wind, her walking stick raised, her teeth bared in anger.

"That's my Cara, that is," she shrieked, giving Levi a tap with her stick. She used all her strength, but the puny blow glanced harmlessly off his arm. "Don't you dare hurt her, or I'll eat you alive."

Glen made a move toward the old woman, but Cara held up a hand. "Stop!" she cried. "Please – she's with me."

"I'll gut you," Livia threatened, brandishing her stick.

"Livia." Cara laughed through her tears, gripping the old woman's hands. "It's all right. I'm all right. This is Glen and Levi – my..." She met Levi's eyes and smiled. "My family."

"*Levi*." Livia beamed, transforming instantly to happiness. "I thought Cara had imagined you. But you did find her after all."

"Livia," Margaret was speaking, and her tone was strangely shaky.

They all turned. Straightening slowly, her movements stiff, Margaret had lifted something small and shining from the ground. Cara saw that it was the little dried rose in the glass jar.

"That – that's mine," she said. "It's a gift for Betty." She held out a hand for it, but Margaret wouldn't let it go.

"Oh, *Meg*," said Livia.

"What is it?" said Cara, puzzled by the look on the old woman's face. "What's the matter?"

Livia looked up at her, her eyes filled with tears. "That's Vickey's," she said.

"What?" Cara looked at Margaret. "What do you mean?"

"Vickey made these and sold them," said Margaret. "Where... where did you get this?"

Cara's heart gave such a thump that she felt it might have plunged clean out of her chest and run wild through the slumbering streets of London at Christmas.

"I bought it from a flower-seller," she whispered. "A lovely woman with great dark eyes."

"Oh, Cara, do you see what this means?" Livia clasped her hands. "You *did* see your mother one last time before she died. She sold you this rose."

It was all too much for Cara. She turned to Levi, who held out his arms to her, and she flung her arms around his neck. The feeling in her heart was misery and hope, joy and terror, courage and sorrow, and above all, a great pounding tide of love. It wasn't jolliness or merriment, but it was perhaps the closest thing to the first Christmas that Cara could ever have felt.

CHAPTER 23

EVEN THOUGH SOME attempt had been made at decorating the walls of the Middlesex County Lunatic Asylum, Christmas never quite seemed to have reached the bare hallway that Levi and Cara were walking down side-by-side. The holly wreaths on the doors couldn't abolish the strange warbles and frightening cries that occasionally echoed from the depths within. Cara felt a long shiver run down her spine and drew closer to Levi, holding a brightly wrapped parcel tightly under one arm.

"It's all right, love," said Levi. "We won't be long."

"This place is frightening," Cara whispered.

"I know, but it's a good place," said Levi. "Better than some of those other dreadful asylums where they tie the poor people to beds and such things."

Cara supposed he was right, but the asylum still gave her chills. She'd seen some of the people walking around on the lawns or sitting in the common rooms as they'd made their way toward their destination, and the looks in some of their eyes had frightened her.

"Here we are," said the young woman in a plain uniform who'd been leading them down the hall. "This is your mother's room." She smiled brightly. "Thank you for visiting her. We hardly ever have visitors here, you know, and I'm sure she'll appreciate it. She talks about you all the time, Mr. Hall."

"I'm sure she does," said Levi with a thin smile.

The door swung open, and Cara felt her stomach clench as she set eyes on Edna for the first time in a whole year. Cara remembered well how Edna had lost her mind when she spotted Levi leading her through the front door of the manor house on that cold, frightening Christmas exactly one year ago. The woman had fallen upon her, screaming and scratching. Glen had been forced to pull her away and lock her in her room, and not long after that, Edna had been taken to the asylum at Hanwell.

Now, she seemed more composed than Cara had ever seen her. She sat in an armchair, a book on her lap, a handful of birdseed in her palm. Leaning out of her chair, she was trickling bits of birdseed into a canary's cage. The little animal chirped and hopped around its perches, eventually landing on the floor to peck at the treat.

"Hello, Mama," said Levi.

Edna looked up. Her eyes lit up when she saw him, smiling widely. "Levi, darling," she said. "It's so good to see you."

Cara tightened her grip on Levi's arm. He laid his hand over hers. "Merry Christmas," he said.

A shadow fell over Edna's face. "Oh, you know how I hate Christmas," she said.

There was a minute's silence. Then Cara stepped forward, forcing down the fear and hatred in her throat, and chose forgiveness in a simple movement as she held out the gift. "I've brought you something, Edna," she said.

Edna's eyes flickered across her face, and Cara braced herself for a raging outburst. Instead, a vague smile crossed Edna's face. "Who's this nice young lady, Levi?" she asked.

Cara stared at her.

"Ah..." Levi hesitated, then smiled, drawing Cara closer. "Mama, this is my lovely wife," he said.

"A wife." Edna stared. "How long have you been married?"

"Two months," said Levi firmly, "and we're very happy. I love her more than I love my own soul, Mama. She's my whole world."

Cara nestled closer to him, grateful for the encouragement, and watched as Edna's face relaxed into a smile. "It's nice to meet you, dear," she said, taking the gift from Cara. "What a treat."

Cara felt herself relax a little as Edna tore at the bright paper, then pulled out a wooden box. She opened it and lifted out a simple thing: a fine little doll, made from porcelain, her friendly features beautifully painted. It was similar to the row of dolls that sat on the mantelpiece of Edna's room, on her bed, on the coffee table. The care givers had told Levi that dolls were the only things that seemed to calm her.

"Oh, how lovely," said Edna, stroking the doll's hair. "How very lovely."

"We must go now, Mama," said Levi, bending forward to kiss his mother's cheek. "Have a lovely Christmas."

"You too, darling," said Edna, but she didn't look up.

As Levi and Cara headed out of the door, Cara looked back one last time. Edna was still stroking the doll's hair, gazing into its lifeless face.

❧

IT WAS a relief after the cold and bleakness of the asylum to be stepping into the warmth of home. Cara still felt a little awkward, even all this time later, to be walking right up the broad front steps and into the beautiful polished hall of her home. The awkwardness vanished the moment she stepped into the house and Glen came striding across the hall to meet them, the crinkles at the corners of his eyes lifted in a smile.

"My darling children." Glen gripped Levi's hand, then bent to kiss Cara's cheek. "You're home just in time for the loveliest Christmas dinner. How is your mother?"

"She's just fine, Papa," said Levi. "She likes the gift."

"Oh, good. Well, I'll be seeing her tomorrow," said Glen, and Cara saw the sadness in his eyes. It vanished a minute later, replaced by a wide grin as he reached for Cara's hand and cupped it in both of his own. "But let's not talk about her now. Tonight is all about you, my dear girl. Come."

And then they were walking into the dining hall, and it was exactly as it had been in Cara's dream. There was the Christmas tree with its feet buried in brightly wrapped gifts, and the glowing candlelight, and the cards on the mantelpiece from the many new friends Cara had made in the past year. Best of all, there was the table with all its food laid out in shining silver dishes: the golden turkey with its chestnut sauce and stuffing, the great plum pudding, the roast vegetables, the neat rows of pretty crackers, the candles and the holly and the wonder of it all.

Betty was beaming proudly in her cook's uniform, her eyes shining with love and pride; Livia and Margaret stood on either side of her, filled-out and happy now in their roles as Betty's assistants. Cara knew that they didn't really need two second cooks, but Glen had been happy to give them positions in his home.

"What do you think?" said Levi.

"I love it," said Cara. "Oh, it's perfect, perfect. I love it. I love it."

Glen laid a hand on her shoulder. "I'll admit, Cara, I wasn't very sure of Levi's choice when he decided to marry you – and while he was still studying," he said. "I only gave in because I felt obliged to support you after everything our family has put you through. But now, I can see that you are the best choice my son could have ever made."

"Oh, Papa, this is no time for speeches." Levi laughed. "Let's show Cara what Christmas is really all about."

Cara looked up at him, and a surge of love rushed through her, so powerful it took her breath away.

She let out a sound that was part laugh, part wistful sigh. "I think I already know what Christmas is all about—at long last."

The End

CONTINUE READING...

THANK you for reading ***The Little Christmas Waif!* Are you wondering what to read next?** Why not read ***The Seafarer's Lost Daughter?* Here's a sneak peek for you:**

Lindy's heart thumped against the bars of her ribs like a wild animal trying to escape its cage. Each thump sent a fresh shock of pain and adrenalin through her body, and she forced that fear into her legs, making them move faster. Her bare feet slapped on the cobbled street as she ran. It felt as though her lungs were bathed in acid, but she couldn't stop; every time she felt about to flag, her pursuer's cries spurred a fresh burst of speed from her tiring body.

"Come back 'ere!" shrieked the harsh, female voice. "Ye filthy wee scoundrel!"

Her words snapped at Lindy's heels like a lash. Clutching the little pouch of coins tightly in both hands, she bolted around the corner of the bakery and into the town square. Two small figures cowered by the single lamppost, staring as Lindy ran up to them.

"Thief! Ragamuffin!" roared the woman's voice.

Lindy stumbled to a halt beside the two little boys. Rueben was only eighteen months her junior at nine and a half; he looked up at her from under a tousle of golden curls, his blue eyes wide. "Did you get t' money?" he asked.

Lindy shook the pouch, making it jingle. "Everything we're owed," she said.

Aram, aged seven, grabbed at Lindy's skirt. "Listen!" he cried in alarm.

There was a clank from behind them. Lindy didn't have to turn around to know that the baker's wife had just removed the chain from their mastiff's collar. There was a ear-crunching bark, and the scrabble of paws on stone.

"Come on!" she shouted, grabbing Aram's hand. "Run!"

Aram's frightened breaths panted beside her as they all three sprinted across the square. Coarse laughter echoed from the surrounding doorways as the mastiff bounded after them, its baying forcing them to go faster. Lindy's free arm swung as if she could push the distance aside. There was a wall at the end of the square, separating the church garden from the street, and she knew from experience that she could climb it if she was desperate enough. Determination drove her legs faster. She locked her eyes onto the brick surface, ignoring the pain in her legs, and tugged Aram's arm to make him keep up.

They were halfway across the square when she risked a glance behind her. The mastiff was a golden blur of churning muscle, hurtling toward them like a shouted curse. When it barked, its mouth was red and wide.

Click Here to Continue Reading!

http://www.ticahousepublishing.com/victorian-romance.html

THANKS FOR READING

ABOUT THE AUTHOR

Faye Godwin has been fascinated with Victorian Romance since she was a teen. After reading every Victorian Romance in her public library, she decided to start writing them herself —which she's been doing ever since. Faye lives with her husband and young son in England. She loves to travel throughout her country, dreaming up new plots for her romances. She's delighted to join the Tica House Publishing family and looks forward to getting to know her readers.

contact@ticahousepublishing.com